MURDER BEHIND THE GATES

THE PRIVATE INVESTIGATOR ANNIE HUDSON MYSTERY SERIES
BOOK 1

VALERIE BRANDY

EMERALD LION PRESS

Published by: Emerald Lion Press.

23901 Calabasas Rd., Ste 2088,

Calabasas, CA 91302.

emeraldlionpress@gmail.com

ISBN 978-1-964161-13-6

Cover design by Stuart Bache. Editing provided by Sharon Lennon-Mehlschau.

Printed in the United States of America. To request permission to use passages from this book in any context other than a review, please contact the publisher at emeraldlionpress@gmail.com.

Visit the author's website at: www.valeriebrandy.com

Created with Vellum

CONTENTS

DEDICATION

To my Mom, for believing in the promise of these stories.

And to our readers. You are the reason we keep coming back.

CHAPTER ONE

THE STREET where Mr. Markin's body was found was unlike any other. Not because of its shape. Aspen Lane was a common cul-de-sac, flanked on each side by tall trees of its namesake that marked a single outlet serving as both entrance and exit. It wasn't remarkable, either, that the cul-de-sac was protected by a twelve-foot-high, ornate iron gate. In the pristine, lakeside town of Watersborough, Massachusetts, it was fashionable to display wealth disguised beneath utilitarianism. The town's richest residents lived in gated communities, for safety, of course. They drove the latest model Tesla, to reduce emissions, naturally. In this respect, the cul-de-sac was one of many such enclaves. Ostentatious, but practically so.

No, the cul-de-sac where Mr. Markin met his end wasn't special because of its exclusivity (although it was exclusive), or its expense (although it *was* expensive). The cul-de-sac where Mr. Markin died was special simply because of the six families that lived there, and their undeniable differences.

Never in Watersborough had such a diverse collection of humans put down roots. It was by chance, perhaps, that such different people were drawn to the same place, unaware of how their lives would become intertwined. Unusual, considering Watersborough was an overtly homogenous enclave. Odd, that six strangers— five, now that Mr. Markin was gone — had ended up together behind that iron gate, connected by invisible strings. It was enough to make the right kind of person believe in fate.

Private Investigator Annie Hudson was no such person.

As she stood in front of Mr. Markin's body— his arms splayed open in the middle of the asphalt, a mess of a bullet hole carved into his left pectoral muscle— she scanned the six houses that circled the cul-de-sac. The evidence she'd gathered so far pointed to one conclusion:

Someone who lived in one of these six houses killed Mr. Markin.

Each house was a multi-level brick mansion, constructed back in the day when houses were built *right.* Despite their similar origins, each house had changed over time to reflect the tastes of its owner.

The first house was painted a bright, unapologetic pink, a celestial wind sculpture rotating on the front lawn. Beside it sat an immaculate, classic home, flanked by a white picket fence. Next to that house, in third position, was an ultramodern, recently upgraded home that had been coated in exterior concrete to give the impression of modern wealth. In its shadow, in fourth position, was an artistic, modest home with no recent upgrades except an apparent garage conversion, as indicated by large windows in the front from which the entire cul-de-sac was visible. In fifth position was the oldest house on the street, still featuring the original iron fixtures and trim. Finally, in sixth position, sat Mr. Markin's small home, which— judging by the art déco border on the front porch— had been updated once in the early 1970s, then left alone entirely.

Annie took in the homes, wondering at the people within, but not daring to guess. Annie *never* guessed. She dealt only in facts, not suspicions. Although, a suspicion couldn't hurt, when it *led* to a fact.

"The gate operates on plates, then?" Annie asked, so lost in her musings that her voice sounded like that of a stranger.

Beside her, FBI agent Ethan Beckett smiled. He was middle-aged, the corners of his eyes permanently crinkled. Not just from seeing too much, but from finding a way to laugh at it, too. "Just the license plates," he confirmed. "Can't even give out a guest code. Every single visitor to Aspen Lane has to check in with security. Tells you everything about the kind of people who live here, doesn't it?"

Annie nodded. "And the guard was on duty?"

"He was here and came running as soon as he heard the gunshot," Agent Beckett checked his notes. "He made the 911 call. Stayed with Mr. Markin until the cops arrived. Said he didn't see anyone fleeing the scene."

"And the guard is a reliable witness?"

"File says the security company checks these guys within an inch of their lives. Background checks, credit reports, the whole gamut."

"And there's no other outlet?" Annie pressed.

"Just the gate. It records the openings, too. Nobody left. Nobody exited. The guard's list shows no visitors. So..."

"It was someone who lived here," Annie answered, finishing his thought. "That was my initial suspicion as well," she conceded, again considering when suspicions might lead to facts. "But there's only one way to know for certain."

"Report says the guy's house was broken into a week ago," Agent Beckett added. "He called the Police. They did a check. Never caught the thief. Figured it was a petty smash and grab."

"Anything missing?"

"Just one thing," Agent Beckett replied. "A vase in the shape of a flower. Kind of a sculpture. Worth about five hundred bucks."

"Not worth the risk of going to prison, is it?" Annie answered.

"Think the two crimes are related?"

Annie turned, the air somehow crisper in her lungs than on an ordinary day. "That's what I'm going to find out."

"You've always loved this part," Agent Beckett shook his head, unable to keep the glint out of his eyes. "Where do we start?"

Annie bent down, reaching into her briefcase. She extracted a pile of envelopes, passing them to Beckett. He opened the first envelope, unfolding a single page within.

Annie grinned at him. "We invite the residents of Aspen Lane to a neighborhood meeting."

"You sure you don't want to start with one-on-ones?" Agent Ethan Beckett probed, skeptical of her strategy. "Lotta things can go wrong in a group interview."

Annie kept her eyes locked on his, unflinching. "I'm counting on it."

CHAPTER TWO

KRYSTAL

KRYSTAL WAS in the middle of giving a psychic reading when the envelope arrived. She was settled inside the living room of her bright, pink home, which she considered the most energetically pure on the entire cul-de-sac. Because Krystal's house was the first home visible upon entry to Aspen Lane, she took great pride in maintaining its colorful salmon facade.

The interior of Krystal's home echoed its exterior, featuring a bohemian design aesthetic. Brightly colored shag carpets. Woven wall hangings. Books and candles everywhere. In the living room, Tarot cards littered her table. Beside them sat her cell phone, a caller on the other end.

"That's what I'm telling you," Krystal clucked, flipping her long, dark hair over her shoulder. "He's like, totally lying to you. There's no way the seven of swords comes up that many times otherwise."

She tapped her fingers on the table, rings stacked on each one. Krystal's voice had the unmistakable tilt of a California Valley girl. Her tight, crisp vowels exhibited the hallmark tone of a West Coast transplant, but her fashion choices created an elf-like, other-worldly effect. She wore a loose, patterned linen skirt, a sash tied above the waist, and a multitude of braids weaving through her beaded hair. A headset sat on her ears like a crown, connecting her to her tele-client.

"I mean, *honey*," she chimed into the headset, "If he's not the one lying to you, somebody sure as hell is. Like, that's an even scarier thought, right? I think we kind of *hope* it's him."

Muffled protests echoed from the headset.

"No, I'm *not* going to run the cards again, because part of a spiritual life is accepting the truth. Of *course*, I'm reading them right!" Krystal paused, allowing the voice on the other end to interject. "Okay, so I was wrong about the job, but like, the cosmos is always shifting! Plenty of things happen I can't predict—"

As if the universe had been listening, there was a metallic clang from Krystal's front door. The mail slot lifted, an unseen hand pushing an envelope through the opening. It dropped onto the parquet foyer floor, glaringly obvious and unusual. There was no other mail. Just the envelope. The lack of a stamp on the front told Krystal it had been hand-delivered outside the regular postal service. And— as Krystal knew from experience— nothing good was ever hand-delivered. Divorce papers. Debt collection attempts. A court summons. These were the only things one could expect to arrive in such a fashion.

"Uh-huh," Krystal nodded into the headset, the voice on the other end becoming one long, blended murmur. "Exactly, that's a great way to look at it," she added, apparently not listening to her caller at all.

She stood, walking toward the envelope as if in a trance. She turned it over in her hands before carelessly ripping the top open to reveal the flyer within. A single page. Simple text in typed, block letters.

"*NEIGHBORHOOD MEETING, to discuss the tragic death of Mr. Markin, which is being investigated as a homicide. Attendance is required for all Residents of Aspen Lane. 3pm, Tuesday November 2nd, at the clubhouse. The Watersborough Police Department and the Federal Bureau of Investigation appreciate your cooperation.*

Please note, any residents who do not attend will be subject to individual interviews at a later date."

Krystal swallowed hard. On some level, she'd been expecting this. She'd watched as the ambulance arrived. Had seen Mr. Markin's body, splayed out on the concrete as if he hadn't mattered, when of course he had. He had mattered to *her.* In a way that nobody knew. In a way that was secret, and shameful. Especially in a place like Watersborough. Nobody who lived on Aspen Lane was aware of the connection that bound her and Mr. Markin.

And now, more than ever, Krystal intended to keep it that way.

"Honey, can you hold for a sec?" Krystal droned into the headset. The voice on the other end started to protest. "Thanks!" Krystal chimed, pressing a button on the headset to mute her client.

Krystal took off the headset. She ran to the dining room table, dropping the flyer off to the side. She scooped up the tarot cards and shuffled the deck. Closed her eyes. Thought about her situation. About Mr. Markin.

"Does anyone know?" she asked the cards, her voice barely a whisper. She flipped through the deck, her practiced hands sensing the moment to stop. Card after card, until—there.

She pulled a single card from the stack. Flipped it over. On the other side: an image of a woman, sitting between two scales, a sword in her hand. The painted figure wore an expression of inevitability, flanked by the trappings of a court of law. A flag. A judge's lectern. The scales of truth behind her.

Krystal took in the figure, concern furrowing her brow.

She inhaled sharply, the card's name escaping her lips on her subsequent exhale.

"Justice."

It was at that exact moment Krystal knew her life in Watersborough would never be the same.

CHAPTER THREE

JANIS

IN THE SECOND house on Aspen Lane, Janis was making breakfast when the envelope arrived. At least, she was *trying* to make breakfast. Her twin boys played a game of tag in the kitchen, weaving behind the island while their purebred Border Collie nipped at their heels. Every now and then, one of the boys would bump into Janis, and she wouldn't say a word. She'd just stare at the eggs in her hands, wondering what chicken they'd come from, and if the bird had minded very much when she'd been unceremoniously pushed aside by farmers with baskets.

Janis shook her blonde bob, trying to move her hair out of her face. She was used to chaos. She was used to making order out of things. She was an expert when it came to untangling messes that weren't hers. Yes, Janis was good at fixing problems made by others. Fixing problems she'd created herself? That was another thing altogether.

She was thinking about those very problems— the ones she'd made herself— when the doorbell rang. The ring was followed by a slipping sound, and a quick glance at the front door revealed an envelope lying under the crack between the floor and the entryway.

Janis stared at the envelope. Wondered what it could mean. The post didn't come until twelve, and it was much too early for the random solicitor.

"'Gonna get that?" Her husband, Reggie, glanced up from the kitchen table where he sat behind an iPad, contemplating the day's returns. Reggie was an investment banker. The kind who knew the difference between a call and a put, and could short a stock in such a way the entire company would fold in some manic self-fulfilling prophecy as a result of his whims. Reggie had an important job, and Janis raised the kids and made the eggs. This was something they had agreed to many years ago before Janis even knew exactly who she was, or what she was saying "yes" to.

"The envelope," Reggie sighed, as if the point needed more explaining. Janis stared at the egg in her hands, hovering over the frying pan. She knew she should drop it in first, but then— what if the letter took some time to read? The egg might burn. And what if the letter said the one thing she feared most? The thing that would destroy her family, and the only adult life she'd ever known.

Janis took a deep breath. She went to pick up the envelope, still cradling an egg in one palm. She tucked the egg under the fleshy part of her upper arm— clutching it like a mother hen— then ripped open the envelope, heart pounding.

Inside was a flyer. At first, Janis felt relieved. This *wasn't* the worst-case scenario. But as she began to read, sweat gathered under her arms, dripping down the fragile shell of that egg.

"NEIGHBORHOOD MEETING: To discuss the tragic death of Mr. Markin..."

"What's it say?" Reggie called out from the table, not bothering to get up.

"It's a neighborhood meeting about Mr. Markin. About what happened yesterday."

Reggie scoffed, as if what happened was beneath him. "Typical. To a hammer, everything's a nail."

"Tuesday at 3 pm," Janis said aloud, more to herself than to Reggie.

"Interrupts the workday," Reggie sighed, taking another gulp of his coffee. He stood, grabbing the flyer from his wife. Janis was so lost in thought she barely noticed. She just stood in one place, watching their kids play through the picture window. They had moved the game of chase outside, and now the dog was with the children in the front yard, making circles behind their perfectly symmetrical white-picket fence.

"Who chose the fence?" she asked absent-mindedly. "Was it you, or me?"

"Hmmm," Reggie answered, not looking at her. His eyes still scanned the flyer.

"Maybe we should change it," Janis added boldly. "Everyone has a white picket fence. Maybe we need something different."

Reggie folded up the flyer, sighing as if his wife were an exhausting person to be around. "It would be a lot of work to change the fence." He paused, adding. "We'll go to the meeting."

Janis turned, snapping back into the present moment. The egg she'd forgotten about fell from her arm, landing with a splat on the kitchen floor. Yolk oozed everywhere, pieces of shell spreading across the tile.

"You'll miss work," she said, searching for a reason Reggie shouldn't go. "I can go, really, it's no trouble. I'll represent us both."

Reggie waved her off. "Better to get it over with now," he said. "But the neighbors," Janis cringed. "You hate—"

"I don't *hate* anyone," he cut her off. "They're just not our kind of people," he shrugged. "This used to be the right kind of neighborhood. Now," he waved a hand around at nothing in particular. "Here we are."

"I can handle it," Janis said. "You've got more important things to do anyway.

Reggie looked at his wife like he was seeing her for the first time. It wasn't like her, to take such issue with a particular thing. Something about her insistence he not attend the meeting made him all the more determined to go. If Reggie was anything, he was a man who didn't like being told what to do.

"I'm going," he grabbed his briefcase off the table, heading for the front door. He paused at the entryway. Turned to face her. "I'll see you there."

He opened the front door, closing it behind him with a thud. Janis wasn't sure if she imagined something ominous in Reggie's tone, or if the exchange had been an ordinary one. She wondered if he knew what she had been thinking about while she tried to make breakfast. Wondered if he could somehow sense the awful thing she'd been hiding. The big mess she'd made that she couldn't clean up.

She watched through the window as Reggie walked down the front lawn, waving at their two boys, who were still playing with the dog. He opened the gate, letting it slam back against their white picket fence.

It was at that moment Janis realized she hated that fence. She wanted to paint it purple or drive over it with a tractor. She wanted to pull it up one stake at a time, freeing the lawn, inviting anyone who passed to enjoy the feeling of grass beneath their toes. But mostly, she wanted to change *something* in her life, even if it meant burning down everything. If only she could find the courage.

Instead, Janis grabbed a paper towel. She bent down to the splattered egg by her feet and started the necessary, painful process of cleaning up her own mess, one bit at a time. As she threw the paper towel away, she thought about poor, deceased Mr. Markin, and wondered if he'd ever felt this way. Like a prisoner in his own life.

If he did, he'd never told her. Janis had always been uncomfortable with the fact Mr. Markin knew more about her than she did about him. Mr. Markin had been a nice man in his eighties, but he was also the type to notice things about people. As horrible as it was to admit, it would be better for Janis if the entire issue of his death would simply go away. And although she'd never admit it out loud—although she'd play dumb if confronted, to protect what was most important to her, the truth was—

Janis knew exactly how Mr. Markin had died. Because she'd seen the whole thing happen. She'd watched his blood ooze over the pavement just like that egg. And although she was sure the memory of his death would stay with her forever, she knew she'd never tell a single soul as long as she lived.

CHAPTER FOUR

JARED

IN THE THIRD house around the curve of the cul-de-sac, the residents were standing on the roof when their envelope arrived. Jared was twenty-two, and handsome enough. He stood at the edge of his home's flat, contemporary roof, looking down at an expansive infinity pool. Unlike every other home on Aspen Lane, Jared's house was coated in cement. The exterior had been redone to make it look like a new-build, and the interior was remodeled with the finest of finishings. Of course, Jared didn't appreciate any of this. He was young, and a Tik-Tok star, who had paid for the place in cash. He bought it because he knew he could afford it, it was the best thing on the market, and Jared loved having the best.

Right now, he was about to earn his keep. Beside him, his two brothers— Edmonte and Marcus— held a video camera and a sound recorder, respectively, each pointed toward Jared.

"What do you think guys?" Edmonte spoke into the camera. "Can Jared survive the fall, or is this the end of our channel?"

Jared and his brothers ran a social media channel based entirely on Jared doing stupid things. Running marathons in high heels. Rock climbing while blindfolded. The three entrepreneurial brothers had made a way for themselves in the world simply by being brave, and just a little bit dumb. And of course, by recording it all for the world to see.

"This might be my last," Jared confirmed, seriously. He turned around, revealing to the camera that his hands were tied behind his back. "If I don't make it, keep watching my brothers do stupid shit. They'll carry the torch, homies," Jared said, even though he knew they wouldn't. Jared was the daredevil of the group, and the money was made on his back alone.

With that, he backed away from the edge of the roof and crouched down, preparing to sprint. But before he could make a move, the sound of their front doorbell echoed through a nearby bedroom window.

"Should I get it?" Marcus, the youngest brother asked, his innocent eyes clouded and unsure.

"Nah, keep rolling," Jared shook his head.

"Hey," Edmonte said, turning the camera back toward himself. "If Jared eats it, he'll get to see the guy that just died last night in the middle of our street up there by the pearly gates. That's right, viewers, last night there was an actual death and possible *murder* on our very own street. We'll do a whole video on it once we have more information. Leave it to the three stooges to bring the latest drama right to your door. Tune in next week to see video of the cops coming. Right, Jared?"

Jared didn't answer. It was Marcus who spoke first, concern etching his asymmetrical eyebrows. "Maybe that's what the doorbell was about? Maybe they're asking everyone if they knew Mr. Markin."

Edmonte shrugged his shoulders. "Then they came to the perfect place." He paused, for dramatic effect, then added, "Jared and Mr. Markin were *friends.*"

Jared couldn't help it. His stomach turned. He *was* friends with Mr. Markin, but he hadn't realized his brothers knew about it. His oldest brother, Edmonte, had a way of seeing things Jared had wanted to keep to himself. It had been that way since they were kids. And he'd always shrugged away his discomfort with one thing. Humor.

"Friends?" Jared smiled to the camera. "Please— like I have any of those." With that, he ran toward the edge of the roof, tossing himself over the cement edge. His body flailed in the air, suspended in time for a moment before hitting the water at an odd angle. Chlorine rushed up his nose, burning the back of his throat.

Jared struggled against the knots in the rope tying his hands together. Then, an odd, quiet peace came over him. This was why Jared enjoyed doing stupid things. The adrenaline rush provided him a clarity— a calm— that was borderline inappropriate, almost pornographic considering the seriousness of the moment. Jared handled brushes with death like a smile at a funeral. The calm that overtook him always carried him through.

Now, that same calm made him pull at the knots in the rope, a bona fide Houdini finding his way out of the deep end. His feet hit the bottom of the eight-foot pool, and he kicked off, hard, sending himself toward the surface to buy some time. His mouth broke past the water and he sucked in a deep inhale of air, noticing the sound of his brothers cheering overheard. Then, he sank again, pulling at those knots.

As one knot came free, the same calm that guided Jared to the surface made him think about Mr. Markin. Jared wondered why he'd seen police cars outside for so much of the night. He considered the ring at the doorbell. Maybe a police officer was standing outside their house right now, waiting to interview them about their neighbor. Maybe the police knew— like his bother— that Jared and Mr. Markin were friends. Or maybe, even worse, the police knew what Jared had done.

Jared almost inhaled water, thinking about a particular item he had inside their home. Inside his bedroom— at this very moment— sat something that would undeniably connect Jared to Mr. Markin. And maybe, even, to Mr. Markin's death. An undeniable piece of evidence that, if discovered, would change Jared's life forever.

Just then, Jared loosened the last knot. His lungs were heavy as he kicked toward the surface, a lack of Oxygen burning in his veins. He broke through the water just in time, inhaling deep, his brothers' cheers drowning out his desperate cry.

"Could somebody just answer the door already?"

His brothers quieted, staring at each other. Whatever had happened under the water, it must have been a close one.

"I'll get it," Edmonte answered, setting down the camera for the first time all morning.

CHAPTER FIVE

SHEILA

IN THE FOURTH house on Aspen Lane, Sheila was up to her elbows in clay when the envelope arrived. She sat at her turn table in the garage conversion with the big windows, watching the brown mud spin around, jazz music playing in the background. She was a pottery teacher, and sometimes an award-winning artist when the wind blew the right way and she made something worth talking about. Her house was two stories like the others and still almost entirely in its original form, except that the garage had been turned into a pottery studio, much to the neighbor's chagrin. The construction alone had just about resulted in a protest from most residents behind the gates. They'd originally planned to skip permitting the conversion, but the uproar from the rest of the neighborhood made such a move impossible. Now, Sheila had her own hard-won studio, with cement floors and windows that looked out at all the people who hated her for it.

As an artist, Sheila rarely liked to involve herself in politics. An export from Australia, she'd left her home country partly because she was tired of being called a "Sheila named Sheila." Everywhere she went, locals knew her as that "Sheila named Sheila!" It didn't help that she was unusually tall for her gender— six feet to be exact. Combined with her tanned skin and bright red hair, Sheila's height made it impossible for her to blend in. In her home city of Melbourne, she was practically a fixture— an icon everyone knew. One step away from being pointed out by tour buses, along with sculptures and museums. That "Sheila named Sheila."

She'd hoped starting over in America— her partner Melissa's country of origin— would mean she could leave the ongoing label behind and for the first time in her life, just blend into the fabric of the world. But when she arrived in the States she felt a new label was applied to her sense of self. It was a well-meaning one, but still limiting, like so many well-meant labels were. Here, she was a member of the "community." She was asked to identify exactly where she fell on the "spectrum," as if where and how she placed her vagina was anyone's business. New, well-meaning friends at her partner's University would ask her if she felt it was harder, "... as an LGBTQ woman," or if she felt discriminated against. Sheila never knew how to answer. All she knew was she'd always been attracted to women, and sometimes just to people, and she was tired of sticking out all the time. She didn't want to be known as that "Sheila named Sheila," but just as herself, and all of that was good enough for her.

The door that connected the studio to the main house burst open. "You won't believe this," Melissa's voice rang out over the jazz music. "They're having a meeting about Mr. Markin." She strode into Sheila's pottery studio, disrupting the equilibrium.

Sheila slowed the turn table. Pulled her hands out of the clay. "It hasn't even been twenty-four hours," Sheila answered, thinking about what she'd seen the morning before. Ambulance lights down the road. Crime tape marking off the street. Poor Mr. Markin, unable to stop them all from looking at him. Sheila knew Mr. Markin would have wanted his privacy. They shared that trait in common. "A memorial, already? Bugger."

"Not a memorial," Melissa shrugged. "An *investigation.* They want to ask us all questions."

Sheila blinked. That *was* unbelievable.

"I saw them drop an envelope through Krystal's mail slot too. You know what that means?" Melissa asked, pulling her blazer tighter around her shoulders. Melissa was a Philosophy professor at the local university, and she liked to wear blazers in her off time to remind everyone that she was an intellectual, just in case they dared forget. "They think someone on our street did it. They think one of our neighbors killed him."

"No," Sheila shook her head, rattled. "It was an accident. Of course it was."

"They don't bring in the FBI for *accidents,"* Melissa said, her tone dripping with a level of disdain she usually saved for her students. "This is *murder."*

"Get stuffed. Nobody here would murder a bloke," Sheila said.

"Please," Melissa answered. "These people are monsters. Remember the hell they gave us because we wanted to convert *our own garage* into a pottery studio? You know they wouldn't have given it a second thought if we were the kind of neighbors they wanted—"

"Only Reggie feels that way," Sheila corrected her. "Don't make everyone Reggie."

"I'm not!" Melissa argued, bristling at the idea. "I seem to remember Frank and Lisa being pretty vehemently against your little— " she waved at the studio. "— space, or whatever."

Sheila sighed. This *was* her space. And Melissa always seemed to find a way to take ownership.

"Pretty sure I was the one who had to deal with legal letters, and the permitting—"

"I know," Sheila conceded, like she always did.

"I'm going to that meeting," Melissa switched topics, dropping the letter on a table by the door. "I am *going* to that meeting, and I'm telling the police what a fucked up place this is—"

"Yes, our two-million-dollar garbage can of a home," Sheila rolled her eyes. The truth was that Melissa's wealthy aunt had gifted them the property after they'd married as an incentive for them to stay in New Hampshire. And now, with the interest rates so high, they were stuck. Anything less would feel like a step-down, but "less" was all they could afford. And as much as Melissa loved her principles, she didn't love them as much as Real Estate and a house she could bring colleagues back to without shame. Sheila sometimes wondered if Melissa was so hard on others because there was some small piece of her that was busy judging herself.

"Point is," Melissa continued, "they deserve to know what kind of people live here. For Mr. Markin's sake."

Sheila had never heard Melissa give one rat's ass about Mr. Markin until now. He didn't interest her. He was, for lack of a better description, rather ordinary in the context of Melissa's world.

"You mean for your sake," Sheila shook her head.

Melissa glared. They'd been fighting more than usual lately. Sheila knew exactly why, but never brought it up. She wasn't ready to end their marriage. And acknowledging the root cause of their fights would do exactly that.

"Why are you *like* this lately?" Melissa whined. "It's like you're never on my side." She paused, realizing. "You don't *want* to go to the meeting. Why?"

Sheila bristled. "Because I don't believe anyone on our street would have killed Mr. Markin, and I know you're going to cause a scene."

"You're used to me causing scenes," Melissa smiled at her.

"That's not it." She paused, waiting. "Why don't you want to go to the meeting with me?" Melissa let the silence hang in the air.

Sheila stared at her. One thing about Melissa was that she almost always managed to get her way. She'd gotten her way when they were deciding where to live, and Melissa's hometown was the only choice worth discussing. She'd gotten her way when they'd decided to try for a baby, and Sheila had agreed to stay home because she made less money. And she'd get her way with the meeting, too. Because Sheila always did what Melissa wanted. It was what kept the engine of their relationship running.

"Fine," Sheila said. "We'll go together."

Melissa stepped behind Sheila and wrapped her arms around her shoulders, kissing her cheek. "Thank you," she whispered in the way she had— the one that made her impossible to say "no" to. She paused, then:

"Also, make sure you wear something nice. Not the, you know, overalls," she glanced up and down at Sheila's favorite jean one-piece.

"You're embarrassed by me?"

"Don't be so soft," Melissa rolled her eyes. "I just don't want them thinking we're less than them. Covered in pottery stains. The trash next door. I can hear it now."

"A vivid image. Good on 'ya," Sheila said, annoyed, and a little desperate to get back to her wheel. "Mind if I ... ?" She motioned at the lump of clay in front of her. It was just starting to look like a bowl.

Melissa nodded and skipped out of the studio, fully aware she'd won this battle. She won most of them.

Sheila started the turn table again. Watched as the mud spun around. She thought about Mr. Markin and how he'd ended up in the middle of the street on display for everyone to see. She knew how it felt, to always be looked at. It was a feeling Sheila avoided and Melissa craved. Melissa *loved* all eyes on her. Sheila just wanted the right eyes to glance her way— nothing more, nothing less.

She had lied to Melissa when she said she didn't want to go to the meeting because no one in the neighborhood would have hurt Mr. Markin. If she was being honest, Sheila would have told her partner that there was another reason she didn't want to go to the meeting. It wasn't because she knew Melissa would cause a scene, although that was part of it. Sheila didn't want to go to the meeting because she knew there were two people in the neighborhood who knew exactly what had happened to Mr. Markin.

And Sheila? She was one of them.

CHAPTER SIX

FRANK

IN THE FIFTH house on Aspen Lane, Frank Havvendish was researching the legality of fireworks when the envelope came.

He had lived on Aspen Lane all of forty years. He was seventy-two and grey, but still charming— at least, his wife Lisa seemed to think so. As a retired attorney, he liked to keep busy by engaging in the practice of law when he thought it might help the community, or perhaps someone in need, or maybe, even, his son— Malcolm.

Lisa and Frank had only been blessed with one child. Malcolm was in his mid-thirties and lived with them in the spare bedroom. The three of them were a fixture on Aspen Lane. They had been there so long they were as immovable as the houses themselves. Malcolm had left for a while but had recently moved back in. Frank felt a warm nostalgia at having him home.

In their sunken living room, Frank scrolled through a database search, looking for any law that might prevent the neighborhood from organizing their yearly Firework extravaganza in honor of the holiday season.

Frank hated loud noises. They never used to bother him,

but now, with what he'd learned about the world and its unkindness, loud noises broke his heart in a way that wasn't easy to explain to anyone else. So, instead of trying to explain, Frank instead hoped to use the law to fight his cause. It had never failed him before. Except for when he had tried to stop their new neighbors from converting their garage into some kind of "pottery studio," but that was one battle lost in a long list of wars.

He was thinking about the law and how much it had gifted him when an envelope slid through the mail slot on his front door, right across from his desk in the living room. He paused. The mail wasn't due yet. He stood, walking over to the envelope and picking it up to examine the exterior more closely. It didn't have a stamp and showed no sign of an address.

Frank opened it, sensing the worst. As he read the flyer, his brow furrowed. As if the sound from the sirens last night wasn't enough, now— his family had *this* to deal with.

Frank sighed. He returned to his laptop, closing the search on past court rulings regarding fireworks. He typed into the search bar:

"Criminal defense interrogation strategies."

Better safe, than sorry.

CHAPTER SEVEN

IN A BACKROOM of the Watersborough Police Station, Private Investigator Annie Hudson and FBI Agent Ethan Beckett sat among stacks of files. Cabinets lined the walls, and a busted table balanced on three legs.

"It's the best we could do," Chief Hardgrave said, glancing around the sad excuse for a room. She was a sturdy woman nearing retirement, and she moved through the world as if its presence were an imposition. "Probably not what you're used to at the *Bureau*—" she said to Ethan alone, the corners of her mouth tightening.

Ethan shrugged his shoulders. "This is top of the line," he said, accidentally taking the lie so far that it sounded like an insult. "It's great for us. More than enough."

Chief Hardgrave offered a terse nod, then plopped another file down in front of Annie, who was seated at the table in a prim, upright stance, as if she were attending the county's finest tea party. "Here's all we have. You can use the station. We'll be conducting our own investigation, but I've recently been informed this investigation falls under FBI jurisdiction, so—" Lieutenant Hardgrave waved a hand in the air instead of finishing the sentence, and Annie got the distinct impression she'd been about to say something rather rude but then thought better of it.

"We're happy to cooperate with Watersborough PD in whatever way necessary," Ethan assured her.

"Problem is, this is a small community," Chief Hardgrave said. "Residents will want to see action taken. I'm an elected official," she added, as if to clarify. "This position I have here... I don't take it lightly. And I answer to voters. If they feel a murder happened in one of our finest gated communities and no one was brought to task for it, I can expect a rough election cycle. Understand?" Her question seemed rhetorical, leaving Annie and Ethan to offer nothing but a nod in agreement.

"Good," Chief Hardgrave continued, apparently satisfied. "You do your investigation, and we'll do ours. If you feel you have a strong lead, I hope you'll bring it to us. Otherwise," she sighed, "Try not to interfere."

With that, she exited, the metal door closing behind her with a bang.

"Friendly," Ethan laughed. He was unbothered by the rough exteriors of local police. He'd seen the way they felt a certain ownership over their districts, and could understand the infringement presented by the FBI's arrival. "I don't think we'll have much time with this one. She'll be looking to make an arrest, and fast."

"Best get started then," Annie grinned at him, opening up the file in front of her. "Let's lay out the facts."

"Mr. Markin was murdered behind the gates," Ethan read from his own mirror copy of the file. "The records from the gate company show that no one came in or out that evening."

Annie stood, her legs carrying her around the room in curving directions as if she were a top carving a spinning pattern into the floor. She took her copy of the file with her, reading from its pages for an assurance of accuracy, even though she'd already committed it to memory. "That's a fact the guard confirms," she added.

"Otto," Ethan agreed. "The police interviewed him first. He was the one who made the 911 call after he heard the gunshot. The guards from this security company have to pass an extensive background check, and a lot of them have military service. He recognized the sound right away and came running."

"We don't know *why* Mr. Markin was walking across Aspen Lane. Did someone lure him outside? It's hard to imagine the killer knocked on his door, and that Mr. Markin willingly moved into the center of the cul-de-sac. And, why would any murderer choose to commit their crime out in the open? Wouldn't it be more efficient just to shoot him in his house?"

"Direct," Ethan murmured.

"Killing him in the center of the cul-de-sac feels like a statement. They made sure he was visible to the entire street, splayed out for all to see, even at risk of being seen *themselves*. Unless..." Annie paused, considering. "Unless Mr. Markin was already walking across the street for some reason, and the murderer was an opportunist, lying in wait for the perfect moment."

"Makes sense. Less about a statement and more about seizing the moment."

"That brings us to the murder weapon," Annie said. "Mr. Markin was shot by a vintage handgun—"

"A Colt 1911. Standard issue in the 1970s," Ethan elaborated.

"The gun hasn't been located yet. But it only took a single shot, executed at relatively close range."

"Coroner's report states the shot was likely fired within twenty-five feet of Mr. Markin. This wasn't exactly a sniper operation."

"Which means, whoever killed him was able to get close

to him. Supporting the idea it was someone he trusted. Like one of his neighbors."

"Someone who lived behind the gates," Ethan agreed.

"And then there's the matter of the robbery," Annie continued her pacing, making yet another circle around the wobbling table. She stopped to push a pile of boxes underneath, correcting the table's slant. "A mere one week before he was murdered, Mr. Markin's house was broken into. A window was broken," Annie reached for a file on the table, removing a that featured a time-stamped image of broken glass in the middle of a front-door window. "But otherwise, the property was unharmed. The thief entered, and instead of taking jewelry, money, antiques, or any number of valuable items Mr. Markin was known to have possessed, the thief took..."

"A vase," Ethan rolled his eyes. He read off a police report in front of him, shaking his head at the inadequacy he saw within. "A vase in the shape of a lily. The officers reporting barely filled out the report. They marked it low priority and didn't think it was very serious, given the vase wasn't worth much."

"I wonder if they're taking it seriously *now?"* Annie mused. "Alright, so we have the murder, and the break-in the night before, and then, there's this…"

She reached into her briefcase, pulling out a white envelope. She plopped it on the table, a strange divider between herself and Ethan. The two of them stared at it. Ethan scooted back in his chair, increasing his distance from the object of his disdain.

"The way I was hired," Annie said, more to herself than to Ethan.

"Annie," Ethan answered, his voice quiet. He'd seen the envelope before, but it still affected him. He glanced at a security camera in the corner of the room. Then, he stood, thinking better of himself. He strode toward Annie, turning his back to the camera so that his face couldn't be read. "Do you think it's the same as last time?"

The white envelope lay on the table, the two of them looking at it like it was a bomb that needed dismantling.

"I don't know," Annie answered. "But if it is, it could mean all hell breaks loose. We could be facing something much bigger than we've ever—" Annie stopped herself. Then added, simply, "I'm ready." She stared at Ethan, eyes wide, not a flinch to be found in her carved features. "Are you?"

Ethan let his hand touch hers, just enough that it could have been an accident. As quickly as the moment arrived, it passed.

"Are you kidding?" He grinned at her. "Of course I'm ready." There was a long pause, as he let the point of it all sink in. Then:

"I'm with you."

Annie let Ethan's words sink deep into the part of her that normally pushed people away. She wondered if the past had truly come back to find them, and— if it had— she wondered if the connection they'd built would be enough to protect them both from what was to come.

CHAPTER EIGHT

ANNIE STOOD, arms crossed, at the entrance to the neighborhood country club. It was three streets down from Aspen Lane, situated at the intersection of a dozen similar gated communities. The country club owners had leveraged the local wealth to create a complex available only to residents with the right zip code. It boasted private tennis courts, a trimly maintained golf course, and the opportunity to network with a similar kind of person. Clean grass butted up to stone and marble walkways, pillars holding buildings up like sacred spaces in Ancient Greece.

"Ostentatious, isn't it?" Ethan nodded at a tiered water fountain that stood in the center of the grounds, featuring sculpted angels spitting spouts of water into the sky.

Annie shrugged. "I've seen better."

"Do you expect full attendance?" Ethan probed, a small smirk etched across his imperfect features. Annie had always found him handsome, especially when she noticed the way his face was just the tiniest bit asymmetrical. "It's a fine affair, after all. The talk of the town."

"Full attendance would be surprising," Annie replied

evenly, "What we don't see will tell me more than what we *do* see."

"You have a hunch already?"

"I don't do hunches. Only facts."

"I've seen you make some choices on nothing but a hunch," Ethan added, suddenly somber. "Hopefully ones you don't regret." There was a question in his tone. Annie flinched. She tried, whenever possible, not to make her business personal. But with Ethan, it was always personal. They tried to avoid the subjects of their investigation inferring a relationship between them, but the truth was— they'd known each other for years, and they'd crossed some lines, together. And when all the crossing was done, Annie liked to step right back over the lines to the distance she found most comfortable.

"Not sure if I can say I regret anything," Annie answered lightly. "But it's better not to look backward, don't you think?"

Ethan was stung but recovered quickly. "Except for when the past comes looking for *us.* Annie," Ethan touched her arm. "If this case *is* the same as last time, tell me as soon as you know. Let me inside that brilliant mind of yours. You're not alone in this. It matters to me too. That case— it changed everything—"

Annie shivered. Tried to bury the images that rose to the surface of her mind, uninvited files pouring out of a box she kept tightly shut.

"Each case stands on its own," Annie said. "Until it proves it doesn't."

Ethan shook his head. "Stubborn," he said. "Just like when we were kids." He stared into her eyes, solving puzzles, there. "Part of me hopes this *is* related. For your sake."

"For *my* sake?" Annie bristled.

"You're a genius, Annie. But there's only ever been one puzzle you couldn't solve. If you could solve it, maybe there'd be room for something— more."

Annie clenched her fists. She hated being seen this way, so clearly, by someone who had known her before she even really knew herself. That was the kind of connection she shared with Ethan. A painful vulnerability that was both comforting, and alarming. All she ever wanted was to pull closer to him, and yet— all she ever did was run away.

As if timed to rescue her, a bright pink van pulled up in front of the Country Club, its owner stepping out and luxuriously handing the keys to the valet. Krystal flipped her hair over her shoulder, a picture of bohemian beauty, her flowing skirt out of place in the trim, perfect county club. It was no surprise Krystal's van was pink, just like her house. She liked to present herself to the world as one cohesive "brand" of a person.

"Our first victim," Annie nodded at Krystal, her heart pounding, blood simmering. Annie always got this feeling when she was starting a new case. It was the eager excitement— an almost vengeful pleasure— that came with the chance to take something wrong and turn it right.

Ethan observed Annie tracking Krystal, her full focus turned away from him, like it always did when there was a mystery at her feet. Ethan wished, for a moment, she would see the mystery in him. But Annie wasn't that kind of woman. And he loved her for it in the same way many people loved their greatest vices— carrying a feeling both unconfessed and incurable. A feeling he couldn't admit to, but also, couldn't control.

Ethan looked away from Annie back at the valet, trying to focus less on her and more on the case in front of him. Three more cars pulled up behind Krystal, giving the pair plenty to study. A Maserati belonging to Jared, the new house at the end of the street. A BMW owned by Reggie, the owner of the traditional home at the edge of the cul-de-sac. One by one, the neighbors arrived for questioning, not a single one of them aware of the trap that had been laid.

The group assembled in a conference room stationed in the back wing of the country club, located just behind the white tablecloth restaurant the club boasted about in brochures. It was a small meeting place fringed by overwrought wallpaper. Folding chairs were arranged in a semi-circle, giving the feeling of an Alcoholics Anonymous meeting, or a self-help conference.

"Like, welcome to group therapy, am I right?" Krystal smirked from her seat.

Annie scanned the motley crew of potential suspects, looking for reactions. The neighbors had arranged themselves in the same order in which their houses fell, as if they were unwilling to associate with one another in any other format. Krystal, as the first house on the left side of the cul-de-sac, sat in a chair at the western edge of the semi-circle. Beside her sat her conservative neighbors, Janis and Reggie, both dressed in well-ironed, button-down shirts. Despite their manicured appearances, Janis and Reggie looked a little lost, as if they could not coexist outside the confines of the white picket fence that encircled their home.

Next to Janis and Reggie sat Sheila and Melissa, the same-sex couple that had just moved in twelve months ago. Melissa had her arm around Sheila, pulling her close, glancing at Reggie every now and then to clock his judgmental expression with a joyful smirk.

Beside the two women sat Jared and his brothers, who had been revealed to Annie in a background check as Marcus and Edmonte. Annie immediately associated them with the modern home at the center of the cul-de-sac. Jared's designer jacket and solid gold necklace were much like the house itself — designed to get attention.

Finally, next to the boys sat an older couple, Frank and Lisa. Annie's research had told her they led quiet lives as upstanding members of the community. But their adult son, Malcolm, who lived with them, was suspiciously absent. A detail Annie didn't miss.

"Thank you all for coming," Annie smiled.

"Didn't give us much of a choice," Reggie snorted. Beside him, his wife, Janis, shifted in her seat. Annie noticed the way she shrunk herself down at any sign of irritation from Reggie, as if making herself smaller might abate the problem, or at least enable her to hide until he made a full recovery. "What are your qualifications, anyway?" Reggie continued, looking Annie up and down like she was a flea on a rat. "*He's* FBI," Reggie motioned to Ethan, who stood behind Annie in all black. "But what are you?"

"I'm a private investigator," Annie answered patiently, her voice almost cheerful. She made an intentional effort to appear unaffected by Reggie's inquisition, although the tone behind it certainly hadn't gone unnoticed. In fact, nothing went unnoticed as far as Annie was concerned. She had a special ability to catalog human behavior— every glance, every look, every nervous tic. "I'm certified and licensed through the Bureau of Security, and I also have a Real Estate license. I deal predominately in cases that involve murders occurring in high-profile properties, commercial real estate, and privately held land developments."

"Do a lot of *murders* happen in Real Estate crime?" Krystal asked, blinking her eyes with concern.

"It's a niche," Annie admitted. "But you'd be surprised how often the environment has to do with motivation. That's half the battle, in closing a case. You have to understand why someone would do what they did, and profile the exact kind of person who would commit a given crime. Understanding people is key, and people are influenced by the environment in which they live."

"We don't owe you anything," Reggie reclaimed the

forum, his voice rising. The air in the room seemed to thicken. "You're not even really law enforcement."

"But *I* am," Ethan said over Annie's shoulder, an edge to his tone. "This case falls under the official jurisdiction of the FBI, and we've agreed to work with Annie as our outside specialist. She's being modest, by the way. Annie's the best profiler on the Eastern seaboard. We bring her on to any case where we think the motivation may have been connected to property. But if you don't care to participate, I can always set up a more formal discussion back at headquarters."

Reggie weighed the moment, then shook his head. Satisfied, Annie continued.

"As some of you may know, Mr. Markin was murdered around midnight on Sunday evening." No one spoke. The neighbors glanced around the room, their eyes darting between Annie, and each other.

"He was shot once on the left side of his chest," Annie added. "Forensics on the bullet confirms a single shot from a vintage Colt handgun. Quite devastating. Which brings me to my first question today." She waited a beat, for dramatic effect. "Did anyone in this room hear the gunshot?"

All around the semi-circle, heads shook. Krystal answered first, her expression solemn. "At midnight I would've been meditating. It's very important, for creating psychic connection," she leaned to the side, reaching over her chair to pat Annie's arm. "Like, one girl to another, I totally respect you for what you do, you know, as far as profiling people goes. I relate because I have to delve deep into the human psyche as well." She straightened, looking proud of herself, the added regally, "I'm a tarot card reader," she pulled out a business card, passing it to Annie. "If you ever want my services—"

"She doesn't," Melissa, ever the intellectual, rolled her eyes.

"So you didn't hear the gunshot because you were meditating?" Annie confirmed with Krystal.

Krystal bristled, looking rather offended that Annie hadn't shown more interest in her spiritual vocation. "Yes. I wear noise-canceling headphones with white noise in the background. It's a sensory deprivation exercise. I actually blindfold myself too, to shut out the exterior input of the tangible, non-spiritual world—"

"We get it," Reggie cut her off. "You're special." He turned to Annie. "I was asleep. Didn't hear a thing. I sleep with earplugs in."

Annie nodded. Looked at Janis. "Is that true—" Annie glanced at her clipboard, pretending to be looking for a name even though she had already memorized each neighbor's name, address, and personal profile. "—Janis?"

Janis was startled, almost as if she was surprised anyone noticed her. Then, she confirmed, "Yes. We both sleep with earplugs in. We have a noisy condenser outside the bedroom window. The earplugs are so effective, we don't hear anything. We each barely know the other person is even there." Janis stopped herself, almost as if she'd said too much.

Annie moved on, seemingly satisfied with Janis' explanation. At least, for now. "And what about you two?" She smiled at Sheila and Melissa.

"We were otherwise occupied," she placed a meaningful hand on Sheila's leg, staring right at Reggie. "We like to play music when we have sex." Across the circle of chairs, Reggie's face turned red. "It was pretty loud. The music, I mean. But also us."

"And you?" Annie stopped at Jared and his two brothers. Jared shrugged his shoulders. "Video games. We play mortal combat. Even if we'd heard the gunshot, it wouldn't have sounded like it was coming from the game."

Annie nodded, her gaze falling on Frank and Lisa. "My last witnesses," she smiled gently, signaling she meant them no harm. "Don't suppose you heard anything?"

Frank shifted, uncomfortable. "We had a contractor come

by not too long ago to double up on the insulation. Our house is as sound-proof as we could make it. Double-paned glass windows. Insulation in every wall. We don't hear much, and we—" he paused. "We prefer it that way."

"Thank you," Annie said to the group. "That was very helpful. Next question: Did anyone see anything strange when Mr. Markin was robbed last week?"

A silence settled over the group, as if the robbery were something shameful, not to be spoken about. Watersborough was a wealthy enough enclave that the residents exhibited an uncurable cognitive dissonance when it came to acknowledging their own luck. They were rich, yes, but most of them were the legacy of a family investment. Many of them had worked hard throughout life, true, but not hard enough to have afforded such a lifestyle without a leg up to begin with. They were conflicted about their ostentation and aware of their privilege, but not too willing to do much about it. Robberies and crimes of the lower class only brought that internal conflict to light.

"I saw it in his cards," Krystal contributed, eager to end the uncomfortable silence. "During his weekly reading—"

"You read for Mr. Markin every week?" Annie probed, suddenly curious.

"Ye— yes," Krystal stammered, seeming to intuit that she'd stumbled into something she should have left alone. "He liked to come by every Wednesday."

"How much did you charge him?" Annie asked, mulling over the details. She had already performed a complete psychological profile on Mr. Markin. Based on what her research had shown, he was a financially conservative man, who had made wise investments over time. He was also religious but not spiritual. A regular Methodist churchgoer. As ex-military, Mr. Markin had lived his life with a regimented, disciplined governance. He wasn't the type to throw away hundreds of dollars on multiple psychic readings each month.

"I— well, I didn't," Krystal huffed again, defensive. "I mean, like—" she paused, looking for a reason. "He was my neighbor. I totally couldn't charge him. I told him it was always on the house, whenever he wanted."

"Hey, no fair!" Edmonte exclaimed, outraged. Beside him, his brothers nodded. "You told me it would be $500 when I asked you to see if making Jared climb Rainier Rock blindfolded would kill him or not! You were gonna charge me half a grand for an hour, and you've been giving Mr. Markin free readings every *week*? Jared, tell her how fucked up that is!"

Jared pulled his designer jacket tighter around his shoulders. He wished his brothers would be quiet, and just allow him to blend in for once in his life. He noticed the detective, Annie, watching him, and tried not to make eye contact with her. He had the feeling she was the kind of person who could see straight through you, and he hated it.

"It's whatever," Jared shrugged his shoulders.

"Well," Krystal clucked, enjoying that someone felt deprived of her attention. "Maybe Mr. Markin got free readings because he doesn't throw wild parties at all hours of the night and day—"

"We have the right to rave," Edmonte countered, stopping at a shushing sound from Jared.

"What did you see, in his cards?" Annie asked, motioning for Krystal to continue.

Krystal grew somber. She closed her eyes and put her hands out in front of her as if remembering the feel of the cards beneath her fingers. "I saw deception. I told him someone close to him was presenting a false facade. That his space would be violated. And then, a handful of days later, the robbery happened." She sighed, as if deeply moved by the tragedy. "It's difficult, being able to see the future but being unable to intervene."

"Thank you," Annie replied. "Did anyone else see something strange the day of the robbery?"

Again, heads shook, although Reggie looked as if a thought crossed his mind. Annie noticed. "Reggie? If there's something you saw it could be really helpful to us. I bet you have great instincts," she complimented him, utilizing his greatest flaw— arrogance— to gain the information she sought. "You'd be doing us all a favor if you helped crack the case."

"Our lawn furniture was out of place that same day, in the backyard," Reggie answered, "I'm quite particular about the lawn," he added seriously. "I prefer the furniture lined up in an exact arrangement, which makes the most sense, given the position of the sun at the time of day we use it. But when I came home from work that evening, it was scattered everywhere. The lounge chair was tipped on its side. The wicker sofa had been moved into direct sunlight," he paused, remembering what a mess it had been. "It looked as if someone had run through the yard."

"Did you see anyone?" Annie asked Janis.

Janis was about to answer, but Reggie did it for her. "She didn't," he said. "She was home most of the day, but we think it happened while she was out."

Janis nodded, then added. "I went to get groceries. Then when I came home, the backyard was all rearranged."

"Maybe the thief ran through our side gate and out the back to get away?" Reggie posited. "I can't imagine why he'd rearrange the furniture, except perhaps to hide for a while. It's a shame you missed it," he spoke to Janis alone, now. "Maybe if you'd seen it, we'd have all the answers we need."

"No," Annie corrected him. "No, we wouldn't."

"I'm sorry," a voice echoed from the center of the semicircle. It was Sheila, who up until now had been trying not to draw attention to herself. "But our best clue is some misplaced lawn furniture? Bugger," she laughed, her

Australian accent echoing across the conference room. "Not much to go on, is it? Coulda been the wind just as well."

"The *wind* would never push over this furniture. It's a three thousand dollar set!" Reggie exclaimed.

"Well, I guess you solved the case then, eh?" Sheila snorted at him. "Good on 'ya!" She shifted her gaze to Annie. "Can we move on from the lawn furniture? Crikey..."

"We're almost done," Annie added, feeling that she was losing the room. "Only one more point of discussion." She nodded at Ethan. "You can bring him in."

Ethan strolled across the room to a set of double doors, opening them and ushering in a man on the other side. The man was on the shorter side, built like the back of a barn. Broad and serious, his skeptical mouth carving a curved line beneath his mustache. He was wearing a security guard's uniform from Universal Guards, a privately hired company. There was a grizzled, carved quality to the visible muscles that bristled underneath his skin, like his biceps were creatures of their own merely hitching a ride on Otto's arm.

"Otto," Annie waved him over like she'd known him all her life.

"You brought the security guard?" Melissa rolled her eyes as if she doubted he could contribute anything useful at all. "Shouldn't he be like, guarding the community, given that there's a murderer out there?"

"That's the thing," Annie said, pleased Melissa was helping her make her point. "The murderer, I believe, is not out there. The murderer— is in *here*."

Silence settled on the group.

"Tell them, Otto," Annie encouraged him.

"I was on guard the night it happened," Otto said, his voice gruff and perfectly matched to his abrupt exterior. "No one came in or out. The gate was shut. When the gunshot rang out, I went to see what had happened. I was there within thirty seconds. No time for someone to get much further than, well—" he paused as if afraid to insult his employers.

"Than your houses," Annie finished the sentence for him. "Thank you, Otto, you can go."

He nodded, exiting across the room with a confident stride.

"We suspect the murderer is someone who lives in your community," Annie added. "We believe that whoever killed Mr. Markin is a resident of Aspen Lane."

The neighbors glanced around the room as if they were seeing each other for the first time.

"Furthermore," Annie reached into the stack of papers on her clipboard. "Mere *hours* after the murder was committed, I received this anonymous letter hiring me to investigate. It was hand-delivered to my door by a courier who had no idea who had hired him."

She held up a white envelope, just like the ones she had used to invite the neighbors to the meeting. She opened it up, removing a simple handwritten note with three words scrawled across its surface. "Try Aspen Lane," Annie read the single sentence letter aloud. "Three words. That's all it asked of me. My standard fee was enclosed, in cash. Not a small fee, either," Annie continued. "I of course immediately called Ethan at the FBI, and he informed me of Mr. Markin's demise on Aspen Lane, of which he had just been alerted a few hours prior."

"What does it mean?" Krystal asked, for the first time looking unsure of herself.

"It means," Annie explained, "that there's more than one mystery here to solve." She raised her arms like a camp counselor welcoming students to a summer of adventure. "Thank you all, for being here. You're dismissed."

With that, Annie turned on her heel, Ethan behind her. In their wake, the neighbors reeled, struck by the realization that one of them— was a murderer.

CHAPTER NINE

AFTER EXITING THE NEIGHBORHOOD MEETING, Annie and Ethan had ducked into the Country Club's Bar & Grill, treating themselves to overpriced steak sandwiches and a couple of whiskeys, on the rocks. Now, they were sitting in front of two empty plates, staring at the bottom of their glasses.

"You ready to tell me what you know yet?" Ethan asked Annie. He'd known her long enough that he knew she wouldn't reveal her suspicions without first being coerced by lunch.

"I don't *know* anything. I suspect. Not the same as facts," Annie replied coyly, swirling the last of her drink in her glass. "I haven't found evidence worth sharing, yet."

"If that were true," Ethan answered, "You wouldn't be grinning like a Cheshire cat."

"The Tarot card reader," Annie acquiesced. "It doesn't fit her profile to offer sessions for free. She's a money grabber. She doesn't come from the same background as everyone else here." Annie waved vaguely at the room around them. "And she didn't get a house that expensive by doing favors for free. She counts every dime. And she has a record. Multiple lawsuits against her for fraud. She took her ex-husband for all he was worth. She's all about the bottom line. When has a woman like that ever offered *weekly* volunteer work?"

"I'm with you," Ethan agreed. "She doesn't strike me that way."

"No," Annie added. "If she was offering him free readings, there was something in it for her. And Mr. Markin? His profile doesn't connect with her story either. He wasn't a spiritualist. He was religious. That's two ends where her story doesn't make sense."

"Agreed," Ethan confirmed. "And then there's the lawn furniture."

"Yes, I thought that was odd too. Not so much Reggie. He makes sense in that he's exactly who he appears to be. But his wife, Janis? Her body language says she's hiding something. She was uncomfortable when he brought up the furniture. He didn't notice how she felt, of course, because he didn't appear to notice the emotional state of others in general. But I would wager Janis knows *exactly* why the furniture was moved that day," Annie folded her napkin in a tidy square, positioning it over her plate with care. "We have three mysteries to solve. The murder. The robbery. And..." she slowed, as if saying it aloud was painful, "... the envelope. Who hired me?"

Ethan's eyes narrowed. "I didn't sleep last night," he said, distant. "Wondering if this was it. Thinking that fifteen years later, we've finally found a case that will crack what happened in our own backyards wide open."

" If it's not related, I'll be back where I started, but if it is— I'll have to think about it again." Annie trailed off, remembering the newspaper articles. The cameras flashing. A single envelope with a three-word note inside left at the scene of the crime— a crime that changed her life forever. Annie and Ethan were just kids when it happened. Both of them not a day over fifteen. She'd never felt so powerless. And ever since then, she'd focused on becoming someone who couldn't be beat. She'd built herself into the kind of person who could ensure justice. This case presented an opportunity to test the new Annie she'd created— or, perhaps, to destroy her, if things didn't go according to plan.

"I know," Ethan confirmed. "But here we are."

"Here we are," Annie replied.

"So, what's our next move, boss?" Ethan kicked back the rest of his drink.

"Frank and Lisa? Their son, Malcolm, wasn't at the meeting, and they never bothered to address it. I think we need to speak to him."

"On it," Ethan confirmed.

"I also want to search Mr. Markin's house. Can you get me access?"

Ethan reached into his coat pocket. Flashed his FBI credentials at her with a smirk. "I can get you anything you need."

CHAPTER TEN

JANIS

THE CAR RIDE home from the meeting was uneventful. Reggie drove— ranting about the nerve of "that woman"—and Janis sat passenger side, watching the streets of Watersborough become a blur outside her window.

Janis had grown up here. She'd gone to high school just down the road. Had her first communion at the church on the corner. She was well-known in the community, just like Reggie, until she married him. Somehow, being married to Reggie had made Janis invisible. As he went out into the world and made a name for himself, she stayed home, enabling his life but never receiving equal acknowledgement. She'd faded away in her own hometown. Become nothing but a glimmer in the place she belonged. Growing up, Janis was a star cheerleader. Everyone knew about her and her family. Now, she was lucky if the clerk at the grocery store remembered her name.

When they got home, Janis made dinner for Reggie and the boys. She tucked her kids in. Put them in their favorite rubber duck pajamas. Then, she proceeded to the bedroom, where Reggie was already perched on the edge of the bed, removing his watch and placing it on the bedside table.

"Still can't believe that woman thinks *she* can get to the bottom of this," Reggie shook his head. "She's already making a mess of it, treating us all like suspects."

He grabbed for a pair of earplugs sitting in a jar by the nightlamp. Without waiting for Janis' response, he shoved them in his ears, rolling over and flicking off the light.

Reggie had told the truth when he said they wore earplugs at night, Janis thought to herself. But he'd unknowingly lied to the Detective about her whereabouts. Because Janis hadn't been in bed at all the night Mr. Markin was murdered.

Just then, the thermostat clicked on, and the condenser outside the window roared to life. It *was* incredibly noisy, which is why— tired of her husband's complaints— Janis had purchased the earplugs in the first place. She'd gone to Costco that very day and bought two sets.

But as time went on, the earplugs became an enabler for Janis's worst vice. When Reggie had the earplugs in, he was dead to the world, which enabled Janis to sneak out of their marital bedroom without waking him up. Reggie had never caught her sneaking out. Not once. He had no idea his wife had been leaving him alone in the middle of the night. And that's why he'd accidentally lied to the Detective. He didn't know Janis had been taking nights to herself away from their home— nights to indulge the side of herself she kept hidden from him.

The night Mr. Markin was murdered was one of those nights. Janis hadn't been in bed at all.

And because she was a sinner— because she'd been out that night, indulging her vice— she had seen Mr. Markin's murder. She witnessed the entire thing, because she was, as a matter of karma, there when it happened.

Janis knew exactly what happened to Mr. Markin. But she also knew she'd never tell.

Janis rolled over and grabbed her own set of earplugs,

shoving them in her ears, wishing they could drown out the sound of her thoughts. She stared at the wall, afraid for herself. Afraid of what would happen, now that one secret had become two.

CHAPTER ELEVEN

JARED

AFTER THE MEETING, Jared and his brothers had gone to the McDonald's drive-thru for cheeseburgers, but once the burgers were devoured, decided they needed some tequila, too. The desire for tequila led them to Bevmo, at which point Marcus suggested it would be a shame to drink alone. He made a good point, which resulted in multiple text messages being sent, along with some Instagram direct messages, and now— their house was filled with beautiful young people, churning to the techno music being blared through the house's built-in speakers.

Overhead lights flashed red and blue. Jared weaved through the crowd, a red solo cup in his hand. He took in the partygoers. Two women in strapless dresses, perched on the edge of the stairs. A buff guy he was pretty sure played football for the Huskies, leaning against the wall smoking a blunt. All around, high-flyers with beauty or money flaunted both to someone they hoped could move them ahead. Jared didn't even know these people. It was his brother, Edmonte, who leaned into the promise of the life they had all created together. Edmonte was the brains of the operation— the one planning the business moves. Jared was the face of it all— the one who appeared in the videos. And Marcus was the intern — the cheap labor who had hitched his chain to the right wagon, following his older brothers just like he did when they were children.

Across the room, Jared noticed Edmonte sitting on the sofa, his arm around a beautiful woman. Edmonte waved him over. Jared floated toward him, both present and somewhere else, the last hit he took reverberating through his skull like an electric current.

"Her friend wants to meet you," Edmonte shouted in Jared's ear, pointing to the young girl next to him. She was cute, with light brown hair and a toothy smile. She looked too nice. Jared wondered what she was doing here.

"Kate!" The girl called out to her friend, sitting on the opposite sofa. "Look, it's the guy— the one you like, totally love! From Tik-Tok."

The girl on the opposite sofa flushed. She was thin, her hair in braids, little bow clips tacked to the end. She looked to be about college-aged. She stared at Jared with a worshipful gaze.

"Bro," Edmonte leaned in, slapping his brother's arm. "She's all about it. This is the perk of fame. Go make your move."

Jared stared at his brother, then turned back to the girl— *Kate*— sitting on that couch. He should approach her. He should want to get to know her. But something in her eyes was so pristine. It was the way she looked at him, like she thought he might live up to every promise another person had ever made her. It was a glimmer, a star in her eye, and Jared knew that if she got close to him, he would break that star, shooting it across the universe in a cloud of steam and smoke.

He didn't want to do that to her. He didn't want to be that guy. He had never wanted any of this.

Jared stumbled away from the sofa, moving towards the

stairs. He glanced back at the girl only for a moment, seeing the pain in her eyes, hating himself that— even by trying not to hurt her— he had already made a dent.

He reached the bottom of the stairs, pulling himself up the banister one hand at a time. When he reached the landing, he made a hard left, making his way to the master bedroom. He threw open the double doors, revealing a massive room with a balcony and an attached en-suite. He shut the doors behind him, heading to the bedside table. He opened a drawer. Pulled out a baggie of pills. Opiates. His drug of choice. He'd started them after a shoulder injury from one of their video antics, and— despite the fact the pills were first issued under a prescription— had never been able to stop. Now, long after the prescription had run dry, Jared had found new ways to get his fix. With Edmonte's help, of course. Edmonte provided Jared with anything he needed to keep the money machine churning, no questions asked.

Jared put a pill in his hand. Thought about not taking it. But as if it had a life of its own, his hand went to his mouth, and suddenly Jared was swallowing, and the bad thing was done. He could always quit tomorrow— something he told himself for too many yesterdays.

Jared rose, stretching his arms and heading for the balcony, pushing the slider aside so he could get some fresh air. He stood, letting his arms hang over the twisted banister. He looked out over Aspen Lane. When they'd moved here, there'd been a neighborhood uproar. Now that there'd been a murder on the street, maybe the neighbors would realize their parties weren't so bad.

Jared thought about Mr. Markin. How his body had laid splayed on the pavement. He wondered if some part of Mr. Markin was at peace now, no longer having to worry about the troubles of life. Jared wondered if maybe he was happy to have a break from all the troubles of the world.

Curious, Jared reached a foot up to the top of the banister.

Then, the other. He launched himself upward, hands-free, perching himself like a snowboarder on the thin edge of the metal railing. He balanced there for a moment, some small part of him almost hoping the drug would make him slip.

It didn't. He hung there, suspended for a minute, then leaped off the railing with a twist, landing back on his balcony. Jared had always had incredible balance, even as a child. Silly, to think a drug he'd been doing for years could wipe it away. He stumbled back into the master bedroom, landing on the bed with his eyes toward the ceiling, spread-eagled and exhausted.

The private investigator he'd met earlier— *Annie*— had looked at him more than she'd looked at Edmonte or Marcus. It was like she could tell that Jared preferred to hide behind his brothers. As if she knew that he was just a pretty face, and his brothers were the real brains behind the operation.

But she didn't see everything, he thought to himself. He rolled over, looking under the bed for something he'd left there. He reached under the space between the frame and the floor, grabbing something and pulling it toward him with one long, toned arm.

He sat back against the headboard, holding the item in front of him like a baby, or a puppy.

It was a vase in the shape of a lily. It was delicate, made of crushed glass in a Gaudi-style pattern. Blue and purple chips of glass reflected the light back at Jared, and a hole in the top invited flowers.

Jared wasn't sure why he'd chosen to steal this particular item from Mr. Markin's house when he'd broken in last week. He could've taken anything that night. It was quiet, and no one was home. He'd had plenty of time to search the place.

Jared sighed, rolling over, clutching the vase like it was something precious, or rare. Maybe he'd taken it because it reminded him of the way he used to be. It was like the girl sitting on the couch. Hopeful and complete, unaware that people could come along and break you.

When Jared had picked up the vase, he'd made a silent promise to himself that— if he was going to take it— he was at least going to make sure he never broke it. He'd kept that promise so far. Jared was tired of destroying good things. He was tired of being the one who always broke others.

Jared thought about Mr. Markin and what he would say if he knew that Jared was the person responsible for his home invasion. Mr. Markin would have told him the only path to freedom was to turn himself in. He would've said that real men take accountability for their actions.

Jared sniffled, rubbing something wet away from underneath his nose. He realized he was crying, and felt momentarily embarrassed even though there was no one else around to see it. He took a deep breath, collecting himself. Then, he sat up, grabbing a blanket from the end of the bed. He rolled the vase up inside of it, then tucked the evidence back underneath the bed, where he was sure it would be safe.

No matter what Mr. Markin would have said, Jared was on his own now. The private investigator— that Annie woman— didn't know that Jared was responsible for robbing Mr. Markin's home.

And Jared intended to go to any lengths necessary to keep it that way.

CHAPTER TWELVE

KRYSTAL

KRYSTAL WAITED for the sun to set to make her move. It had been a tense afternoon. After the meeting ended, she'd gone straight home and weighed her options, sitting cross-legged on her meditation pillow with her hands on her knees. The private investigator— Annie— had been curious about the fact Mr. Markin didn't pay for his readings. Too curious.

Mr. Markin had assured Krystal the terms of their agreement were private, and she believed him. But even so, there was evidence that could be dug up and claims that could be made.

Krystal waited for the customary peace that came with meditation to set in, but it never came. Minutes passed, or maybe an hour. Krystal leapt up from the meditation pillow, moved to action.

She went to her dining room table and spread out her Tarot deck, reading her own cards again as she waited for evening to arrive. She read once. Twice. Three times. The result never changed. Without fail, the same card appeared in her multi-card spread, like a chant that couldn't be ignored.

Justice. Justice. Justice.

The image of the woman in a court of law, with two scales behind her, resurfaced again and again, leaving Krystal unable to deny what she needed to do. It was a truth she'd been avoiding all along. But now, it was necessary. Undeniable.

She needed to get into Mr. Markin's house, preferably before that private investigator went poking around.

When the sun finally set, Krystal changed out of her typical uniform of a flowing skirt and loose blouse. She slipped on sneakers and a pair of black jeans, topping them with a black sweatshirt. Next, she stood in front of her vanity mirror, donning a black baseball cap, hair tucked underneath. For the finishing touch, she found a black bandana at the back of her closet, tying it around her face to obscure her features.

Outside, sounds of techno music flooded the night air. Krystal pushed back the drapes on her bedroom window, peaking toward the source of the sound: Jared's house. Groups gathered on the home's various balconies, red solo cups in hand. Laughter echoed from the front grass, where a cluster of young people kicked crushed beer cans aside. The three brothers were up to their fraternity nonsense again. At least once a quarter, they'd throw a disruptive party, apologize profusely to the neighborhood the next day, and then hire a cleaning truck to take care of their mess. They were a nuisance that drug down the cultural value the exclusive cul-de-sac held, to be sure. But tonight, they were helping Krystal in an unexpected way. All attention would be on the brothers. The entire neighborhood would be looking toward their house. No one would think to offer Mr. Markin's home a second glance.

Krystal snuck out the front door, the cover of night helping her blend in. Her front patio lights were off, rendering the porch so dark she was sure that no one would notice her lithe form crossing the grass, heading toward the tall trees that lined the entrance to the cul-de-sac. As she sped across the grass, she noticed dozens of cars lining curbside parking in the tiny cul-de-sac, all of them presumably guests at the party. The boys had outdone themselves this time.

When she reached the cul-de-sac's only outlet, Krystal ducked behind a cluster of Aspen trees, waiting. This would be the most exposed part of her route. Before her, the iron gates that protected Aspen Lane were sealed shut. In the guard's station, a single light was on. Krystal strained to peek through the glass divider that kept the guard apart from his subjects. She could just make out Otto's bulky shoulders behind the glass. A landline telephone was up to his ear, and he was waving his arms with urgent fervor. Otto hated when the boys threw their parties, not because they weren't allowed to have guests— they were, unfortunately— but because checking in the many attendees meant Otto couldn't execute his regular routine of sitting in the guard's station, doing nothing except reading his war novels. Otto *loved* his war novels. World War II. The Roman Empire. Fiction. Non-fiction. Otto read it all, as long as it had to do with war. But tonight, he was on the phone, probably making an anonymous call to the police about a noise disturbance in the hopes they would shut down the party, allowing him to get back to his novels.

Just then, a car pulled up to the gates. It was a sleek Lamborghini in a bright yellow color. The driver rolled down her window, revealing a beautiful young girl who couldn't be older than twenty-two. She passed Otto her driver's license with a yawn, and Crystal realized— this was her chance.

After a second glance at Otto to ensure he was sufficiently occupied, Krystal darted across the other side of the gates. The Lamborghini's headlights illuminated her form for mere seconds, but she knew she was safe. The young woman driving the car would assume she was another partygoer, simply crossing the street, and think nothing of it.

When Krystal landed at the opposite set of trees, she tucked herself into the back edge of the property, disappearing into the shadows. She didn't have far to go, now. Mr. Markin's house was only a dozen feet away. Their two homes marked the Western and Eastern edges of the cul-de-sac like two sentinels keeping the community grounded.

Krystal weaved through the trees toward Mr. Markin's backyard, then pulled herself over the short fence, aided by a dead stump in the ground. She landed on the other side in a heap, then brushed herself off. As she headed for the sliding glass doors that led into the foyer, she promised herself she wouldn't get emotional. This was about her future and she knew— she *knew* without a doubt— that if Mr. Markin were here, he would understand.

Krystal pulled, and by some miracle, the sliding door was unlocked. People on Aspen Lane relied on the gates more than outsiders might guess. There was a false security that came with living on a small street, surrounded by people you knew.

Krystal stepped into the house, the distant sound of techno music still thumping in the night. She closed the glass behind her, looking around the living room.

Krystal knew this room well. The dated, cream-colored carpets were familiar, as were the brown corduroy couches that needed a good cleaning. The floral drapes that covered the windows had been purchased by a woman who had lived with Mr. Markin for a few years and then left, taking any sense of style with her. The house still smelled like a faint glimmer of aftershave, although Krystal couldn't pinpoint the brand. This is where Krystal had read Mr. Markin's cards every week. At least, until they'd started fighting and the friendship had soured. She wished he had listened to her when she tried to warn him there was someone in his life he couldn't trust. But of course, he didn't. Mr. Markin didn't believe in anything he called too "woo- woo," and yet, he participated in the readings out of a deep desire to give Krystal dignity. That was the kind of man Mr. Markin had been. A person who always found a way to make somebody else see the best in themselves.

The carpet condensed as Krystal headed down the hallway, stopping to look at a credenza littered with printed photos in neat, tidy frames. There was Mr. Markin in his Marines uniform, a young man, and rather dashing. There he was in his medical gear for Doctors Without Borders, middle-aged but satisfied, looking productive in the middle of a hut with a dirt floor in some unknown place. Another photo showed Mr. Markin with the Key Club, a local chapter of which he might have been President. Krystal wasn't sure if he'd been President or not. She should have asked him, but now, it was too late.

She shook off the sting of some feeling she didn't have time to pick apart, moving quickly toward what she knew to be Mr. Markin's office. She opened the door quietly, as if Mr. Markin was asleep in his bed and might hear her.

The room was sparsely decorated but for a large desk and a filing cabinet. Krystal moved for the cabinet, opening the top drawer and thumbing through file after file. She wondered if other people had made a similar deal with Mr. Markin, and now had no idea he'd never be able to collect.

She paused at a file she recognized. She pulled it out, breath quickening as she reviewed the documents inside. A sigh of relief escaped Krystal's lips. She'd found what she was looking for.

She hurried to the living room, turning the key to Mr. Markin's gas fireplace. It roared to life, blue and gold flames casting light across the floor. When the fire loomed so large it looked ready to consume the hearth itself, Krystal held out the file.

"Thank you," she said in a whispered, final conversation with an old friend.

With that, she dropped the file into the fireplace, watching as the flames turned what was once a threat into nothing but black ash. Krystal waited, patiently ensuring every corner of the offending documents had been burnt into something irretrievable, that card for *Justice* still swimming in her eyes.

CHAPTER THIRTEEN

FRANK

TECHNO MUSIC BLARED, resonating through Frank's traditional home in a pulsating, relentless wave. Every now and then, the plates and bowls that lined their China cabinet would vibrate with a clatter, as if they wanted to jump out of the cabinet to escape the sound.

"Try the police again?" Frank shouted at his wife, Lisa, across the living room.

Lisa nodded, holding up her cell phone. "They said they'd send a car. Otto called too, God bless him."

Frank's biggest wish was that the music from Jared's party would stop. The flashing lights didn't bother him, nor did the menagerie of strangers that flooded the cul-de-sac, parking their cars on the street like ants in a line. Frank could endure any of these elements if only the party itself were kept quiet. As one of two houses at the end of the street, Frank and Lisa were often subject to a kind of noise tunnel that amplified every sound within fifty yards. *Ironic, looking back,* Frank thought to himself. He never would have bought the house if he'd known then what he knew now. Noise disturbances weren't as much of an issue until the neighborhood shifted and new residents moved in. The boys in the most expensive home at the center of the cul-de-sac—Jared, Edmonte, and Marcus— had been a particular problem. But there was nothing to be done about it. They threw party after party, rave after rave. The police came, then left, and the boys would do it all over again a mere month later.

"How is he?" Frank questioned Lisa, asking after his son, Malcolm.

Lisa sighed in response. Shook her head. "I checked. I tried—"

"I'll check again," Frank reassured his wife. He frequently reassured her nowadays, given the state of things. With great effort, Frank rose from his armchair and headed down the hall.

He paused at the door to Malcom's room. It was open. Malcolm sat on his bed, a book of crosswords in front of him. Malcolm was thirty-five and built like a tank. He was all muscle. Malcolm lived at home and spent most of his time doing crosswords or fixing cars for a small sum. He was incredibly capable. The most capable man Frank knew. He was just "going through it" at the moment.

"You good?" Frank raised a hand.

Malcolm looked back at his Dad, moving one of the headphones off his ears.

"No problems here," Malcolm answered. His smile intended to sell the lie, but Frank could see the pain behind his son's eyes. He noticed the way Malcolm's leg bounced up and down as if it had a mind of its own. The way he let the headphones sink back over his ear as soon as possible, returning to his book of crosswords like his life depended on it.

Malcolm had moved back in with his parents to get past his pain, and Frank couldn't help but feel they were failing him every time something intervened with the healing process.

Frank wished they could afford a vacation home or something quiet and small on the beach. That's what this street was supposed to offer Frank and Lisa when they invested in the neighborhood so many years ago. It wasn't fair that it had changed. It wasn't right that the couple had believed in the neighborhood— had invested in the promise of its future— only to be sold a lie.

The only other person on the street who empathized with Frank's plight was Mr. Markin, who had moved in just as long ago and had also experienced changes on the street. Of course, Frank would never have told the private investigator this, but he counted Mr. Markin as one of his closest friends. Frank, his son, and Mr. Markin had gone to the golf course at the country club every week for a game and drinks. Mr. Markin connected with Malcolm in a way Frank couldn't— in a way that was helping him heal. Frank was devastated when he learned of the death of his old friend.

He was also afraid. Afraid that suspicions would be cast on his son, who was already going through enough. People were quick to judge, and a simple summoning of records would allow the FBI to unearth the truth about Malcolm— something Frank was desperate to avoid. That's why Frank had lied about his son's whereabouts the night Mr. Makin was murdered. Frank had told the detectives his son was at home when in reality, Malcolm had been out that night, presumable away from the neighborhood. Frank had no idea where his son had gone the night Mr. Markin was murdered, because he was trying— wherever possible— to give him some dignity and independence. God knew, the man had earned it. All Frank was sure of was that his son had not come home until the following morning. Malcolm was a grown man, and so, Frank had not asked too many questions.

Frank backed away, shutting the door softly behind him, allowing Malcolm to swim in the peace of the puzzles. If only life were as easy to solve as a crossword.

Frank headed back down the hallway but stopped when

he saw his wife, standing at the edge of the landing. The look on her face was desperate, tortured. Frank had been married to Lisa for almost a lifetime, and he had only seen such an expression etched in her features twice, maybe three times before this moment. She walked toward him and clutched his arm in her hand, standing on her tip-toes to whisper urgently in his ear.

"There's something I have to show you," she said, voice trembling. She motioned for Frank to follow her. Together, they marched down the hallway toward the basement, Frank's ears pounding, but not from the music.

"I went down to look for extra towels," Lisa whispered again, as if she were afraid of being found out. "I thought a cold compress might help him," she nodded back up the stairs toward Malcolm's room. "And that's when I saw it."

Lisa pushed open the door to the basement with force, revealing the cold, unfinished shelter. She reached overhead, pulling a hanging string to click on the light. A single bulb illuminated the otherwise forgotten space, which housed a washer and dryer in the corner. Some old planks lay discarded on a table, tossed beside some of Malcolm's car projects. Pieces of an engine. Tools and widgets. Out of anyone in the family, Malcolm spent the most time down here, reverse engineering car parts and radio systems.

Then, Frank saw it. The object of his wife's concern. Against the far wall, a tall cabinet housed a collection of guns. Rifles. Handguns. All of them were permitted of course. All of them were allowed to be here, locked safely behind the cabinet's glass door, their ammunition stored separately. Frank knew the cabinet was here, and took comfort in the ability to protect his home should the moment call for it.

But tonight, something was different. There was a faint outline and two hooks where a vintage Colt 1911 should have been, but the gun itself— was missing.

Frank inhaled. Nobody else had the key to the gun cabinet except for the three residents of his home. Frank. Lisa. And Malcolm.

"The private investigator," Lisa said helpfully. "She said Mr. Markin died from..."

"A single shot from a Colt handgun," Frank finished for her.

As a lawyer, Frank immediately jumped to plausible deniability. He was trained to consider the best-case and the worst-case scenarios. He turned to his wife, the techno music and the party suddenly forgotten. They had bigger problems to deal with, now.

"We tell no one," he said, and Lisa nodded, leaving it at that.

CHAPTER FOURTEEN

THE NEXT MORNING, Mr. Markin's house dripped with a heavy stillness as Annie and Ethan made their way through the foyer. Annie always hated this part of an investigation. She could never shake the feeling she was invading the victim's privacy, assaulting their space as an uninvited guest forcing the victim's hospitality. Still, it was a necessary evil. Annie never learned more about a case than when she rifled through the victim's personal belongings.

"Not great with the home decor," Ethan said aloud, thoughtlessly. "His place looks like mine."

"Don't be rude," Annie scolded. Ethan rolled his eyes. "Yes, we wouldn't want him to ask me to leave."

"It's because he *can't* ask you to leave that you should be respectful. Victims can't stand up for themselves. That's where you and I come in," Annie's voice betrayed a quiver of emotion that Ethan didn't miss.

"Annie, I didn't mean—"

"It's fine," she answered, a little too cold. Annie felt protective over the victims for whom she sought justice, if only because she knew what it was like to never see justice brought to light.

Ethan leaned up against the wall, hands in his pockets as if he was afraid they might betray him if set loose. "You deal with things by taking action," he said, quietly. "I've just learned to joke the feeling away."

"It's alright," Annie melted a little. "It's me, too. It's the envelope, the way this case came to me. It feels like this might be the one we've been looking for—"

"So let's do it right," Ethan held out a pair of plastic gloves. Both Annie and Ethan snapped the latex over their hands to avoid corrupting evidence.

"Where do you want to start, boss?" Ethan asked. "Forensics already did a sweep. Didn't note anything. The police stopped by the night of the robbery, but we all know what good that did. They probably never made it past the front door."

"Let's start here," Annie said, stopping at the credenza in the hallway. There, a set of photos lined the walkway. "I want to know what kind of man he was."

She paused, taking in the photographs. An eight-by-ten showed Mr. Markin with the local Key Club, apparently winning a service award. Beside it, a framed picture of Mr. Markin in a remote village, wearing a uniform, smiling ear to ear. A nametag on his scrubs indicated he was part of "Doctors Without Borders."

"What kind of Doctor was he?" Annie asked Ethan, who checked a pile of paperwork under a clipboard he carried.

"A Dentist," Ethan answered. "Doctors Without Borders has them go abroad to fix kids' teeth."

Annie ran her gloved fingers over a framed photo of a very young Mr. Markin— no more than nineteen years old— wearing an Army uniform.

"He served, too?" She asked.

Ethan nodded, again checking his files. "Served in Vietnam. Honorably discharged. The record shows he was drafted. Seems like he got in, got out, and never looked back.

He became an objector. His only arrest record shows he was at a protest against war—"

Annie pointed to another photo. "Something like this?" The picture showed a young, twenty-something Mr. Markin, surrounded by a group of bell-bottomed protestors stationed in front of a van. They held signs reading *"Love Not War"* and *"Bring back our troops."*

"Something exactly like that," Ethan agreed. "The arrest happened a few months after he left the service. Other than that, the man's got a perfect record. Not so much as a traffic ticket."

Annie's skin tingled. Although she relied on fact over superstition, she also could sense the way the story of a life came together. She could look at the details that made up a person and discern what blocks built them into their current state. She knew that serving in Vietnam had led to everything that was to come, for Mr. Markin.

She paused at another photograph, this one newer. Mr. Markin looked the same as he did spread out on the asphalt — the same age, the same haircut, similar clothes. He was surrounded by a group of men all in a similar demographic, some of them wearing pins on their shirts.

"Look at this," Annie passed the photo to Ethan. "They had a reunion. The date in the corner? That was less than six months ago."

"What kind of reunion?"

"His squadron. Look at the pins they're wearing. Looks like Mr. Markin wasn't completely done with the Army after all. It must have still meant something to him if he bothered to show."

She pointed at the back of the group, singling out a man in his mid-thirties. He was the only young person in the group, smiling ear to ear.

"Recognize him?"

"Is that—" Ethan squinted, rifling through his files. On

one page, driver's license photos of every resident of Aspen Lane stood in neat rows. Ethan ripped off a picture on the corner of the paper and held it up to the photograph. The man pictured looked just like the one in the group photo.

"Malcom," Annie confirmed. "Frank and Lisa's son. Mr. Markin must have brought him to his squadron reunion."

"Why?" Ethan wondered.

"I don't know. Maybe Malcolm will tell us when we talk to him." She mulled over the photographs, trying to visualize the puzzle of Mr. Markin's life. He didn't have children, but he lived his life for others. He volunteered in the community. Gave his time to those who needed it. That was rare, in a man. How could someone so giving— so easy to get along with— merit the rage of another person to the point it escalated to murder? Motives tended to fall into one of two categories: emotional or strategic. Those who killed on emotion were moved by anger or revenge. Those who killed strategically had something to gain, such as money, or an inheritance. Annie considered what motive someone could possibly have against such a man as Mr. Markin.

"Who did he leave his money to?" she asked Ethan.

"He doesn't have any direct relatives," Ethan answered. "The will is sealed, set to be read in a week once Mr. Markin's lawyers finished— whatever it is lawyers do."

"We look forward to that," Annie added, making her way down the hallway.

She stopped at a narrow door, flicking on the light. A small bathroom revealed itself, covered in pink and green tile. A sea-shell style sink dipped low into the vanity, across from a clawfoot tub and a toilet.

"This is the room the vase was stolen from, correct?"

"Yep," Ethan said. "The perp broke into the house, apparently used the John, and left with nothing but a butt-ugly vase. Sounds like a hardened criminal, doesn't it?"

"Sounds personal."

"Exactly," Ethan agreed. "The police took a photo of the bathroom and front door. The notes say Mr. Markin requested as much. Seems they didn't feel it was important."

"I think Mr. Markin would disagree," Annie scoffed.

Ethan passed her a document showing the two points of disruption. First, a snapshot of the home's front door, the glass broken to access the deadbolt. In the photograph, the front door was wide open. The thief hadn't bothered to close it behind him, and neither had Mr. Markin.

A second photo showed the bathroom immediately after the disturbance. Compared to the front door, the damage in the bathroom was relatively tame. A drawer had been pulled from the vanity and left discarded on the tile. Another drawer had been opened and ransacked, its contents spilled onto the rug.

"The thief didn't touch any other rooms?" Annie asked.

"Nothing else."

"They broke in through the front door, and came straight into the bathroom," Annie said, mentally visualizing the thief's trajectory "They didn't stop along the way. Whoever it was, they knew exactly what they were looking for."

Annie studied the vanity. She pulled out the two drawers that had been disturbed in the photographs, removing them from their tracks and setting them onto the rug beneath her feet. She kneeled, reaching a hand into the hole that was left in lieu of the drawers. Her elbow twisted as she reached behind the vanity, exploring the empty space, feeling for the gap between the vanity and the wall.

"It doesn't go all the way back," she said aloud, more to herself than to Ethan. "The vanity. There's a space. It's not built-in."

Ethan didn't ask any questions. He was used to letting Annie think when she was on a roll. And he knew if he *did* bother to ask about her suspicions, Annie wouldn't answer him, anyway. Annie liked to wait to share her conclusions until she had the facts to back them up. Until then— to Annie, at least— it was all just conjecture.

"I've seen enough," Annie announced, pulling off a glove. "I'd like to go outside, to the spot where he died."

She marched out of the bathroom, Ethan trailing behind her. They made their way back through the hallway, curving through the living room. But Annie stopped at the fireplace, noticing the black soot there.

She bent down, touching the edge of what used to be a piece of paper. She raked her fingers through the piles of destroyed records— now turned to ash— feeling rather pleased with herself.

Annie smiled, happy that someone had stepped into the trap she laid. It was funny, how mysteries would untangle themselves if you only prodded the subjects involved to the correct degree. If you let people, they would confess to you in a hundred different ways, both spoken and— maybe more beautifully— unspoken.

"Looks like poor Mr. Markin had another break-in," Annie sighed. Ethan wanted to ask her what she meant, but he preferred instead to marvel at her.

"Poor guy," Ethan agreed.

"Yes," Annie answered. "Let's go see how he died."

And with that, she marched out the front door, the ashen scent of an answer still clinging to her fingers.

CHAPTER FIFTEEN

KRYSTAL

KRYSTAL WAS STATIONED at the lookout, peeking out from behind her living room drapes. She had watched as the two detectives had entered Mr. Markin's home, a nervous knot in her stomach. She felt foolish now, for burning the documents in his fireplace. She should have taken them back to her own home and destroyed them in the peace of her living room, but she'd worried that would incriminate her further.

Krystal had made an emotional decision, to be sure. But gut instincts weren't to be ignored, and that Annie woman's line of questioning had set off alarm bells within Krystal. And Krystal never ignored a higher intuition.

She'd been watching Mr. Markin's house closely over the last hour, waiting for the detectives to reemerge. She half-expected they'd appear with trash bags filled with soot. The idea made her squirm, hating herself for acting so irrationally.

It was the music, she convinced herself. *The music from Jared's house that was to blame.* It set a kind of fever upon her, making her do something she now looked at with regret.

Finally, Krystal peeked out the curtains and saw the

detectives exiting Mr. Markin's front door. They marched across the street, heading in a straight line towards Krystal's home.

Her heart pounded. This was it. They were coming to speak to her.

But then, the female detective stopped in the middle of the road, and her partner lay down on the ground. He opened his arms wide, mirroring the way Mr. Markin's body had been found, completely spread-eagled on the pavement.

Krystal breathed a sigh of relief. She was safe. For now.

CHAPTER SIXTEEN

ETHAN LOOKED up at Annie from the ground, her face warped from the harsh tilt of perspective. "How long am I supposed to lie here?"

"As long as it takes," Annie shrugged.

"And you're going to—" Ethan waited for her to fill in the blank.

"Go for a stroll," Annie answered reassuringly.

"And what if I get hit by a car?" Ethan hated to make a fuss, but some things were necessary. "I feel like you're overlooking an important detail."

"Excellent point," Annie beamed, a little too excited by his suggestion. "You've given me the perfect reason to go check on Otto in the guard's booth. I'll let him know not to allow any cars in. Official FBI business."

"That won't help me if someone peels out of their driveway—" There was a long pause. "Annie?" Ethan sat up. Annie was already halfway to the guard's booth, a pep in her step as she approached Otto within. Ethan sighed, laying his head back down. Might as well wait.

Annie knocked on the door to the guard's booth, grinning

at Otto. He slid the door open. Much to his surprise, Annie stepped inside, welcoming herself into his private domain.

"My partner and I need about one hour with no cars coming through. Can you keep the gates closed?" She asked as if it were a perfectly ordinary request.

"That should be fine," Otto waved her away.

A book sat open on his table. The cover showed tanks. A military operation.

"World War II," Annie noted. "You like war novels?"

"Don't like much," Otto answered. "But have to pass the time."

"I see," Annie answered. She turned, looking back at the cul-de-sac through the windows in Otto's guard booth. From this vantage point, almost every house was visible. Ethan was a mere ten yards away, lying spread-eagled in the street, his hands now behind his head, creating a pillow.

“No furniture in here,” Annie scoped out the space. “Just the desk and those books.” She pointed at the built-in ledge that formed a desk in the booth. Its surface was covered by stacks of Otto’s books.

“It’s not a hotel,” Otto shrugged.

"Thank you," Annie smiled at him. "We appreciate it." She stepped out of the tiny booth, sliding the doors shut behind her like she owned the place. Otto shivered, glad she was gone. He hated it when people acted like they owned a place.

Annie marched back down Aspen Lane, walking past Ethan and heading for Krystal's house. She trampled across Krystal's front lawn, standing in front of the living room window. She stared at Ethan's prostrate figure, ensuring he was still visible. She made a note on a piece of paper on her clipboard, then marched back across the grass.

Next, she headed for Janis's house. She stopped at the white picket fence, opening it and letting it close behind her with a bang. She walked toward the only front-facing window in the house— the kitchen window— and stood in front of it, looking back toward Ethan. She made a note on her clipboard and, when she was satisfied, marched down the street toward the next house, a dog on a scent.

CHAPTER SEVENTEEN

SHEILA

"WHAT THE BLOOMIN' hell is she doing on our lawn?" Sheila asked out loud to no one but herself. She was in her pottery studio, elbow deep in a jar when she'd noticed Annie's lithe figure out the massive windows on the far wall.

When they'd been in the process of designing the garage conversion, Melissa had insisted that Sheila have enormous windows installed to "let in the light."

Sheila had grown to hate those windows. There was no privacy. No peace. All she wanted was to sit at her wheel, unseen by the world. The windows made Sheila feel like she was once again the center of attention, gawked at by all. They faced the center of Aspen Lane, with a perfect unobscured view of the entire street.

Just then, Annie turned around. She waved at Sheila, a bright smile on her face. Sheila noticed Annie's partner laying spread eagle in the center of the cul-de-sac, exactly in the spot where Mr. Markin had died.

Sheila raised a hand in response, tepid and uncommitted. Then, she grabbed a remote control. She hit a button on top, and an enormous set of rolling curtains came down over the glass, slowly obscuring Annie's still-smiling face from view.

What an odd Sheila she is, Sheila thought about Annie, returning to her jar without further delay.

CHAPTER EIGHTEEN

BY THE TIME the hour was up, Annie had stood in front of all six houses on Aspen Lane, mapping their exterior windows for line-of-sight in relation to where Mr. Markin's body was found. The notes on her clipboard were a strange mess of letters and lines, her handwriting— like many other intelligent people's— completely illegible. Diagrams marked the pages, estimating the angle and time of day. Ethan thumbed through it all, trying to get a sense of where Annie was headed with this particular facet of the investigation.

"Are we vetting possible witnesses?" Ethan asked, taking a sip of his coffee. They had stopped at an old, broken-down diner on the outskirts of town. Annie had insisted she wanted an egg and cheese sandwich, but the kind that was made with artificial American cheese. It took a diner to get such a result, and Watersborough was— as they soon discovered— too upscale to offer much in the way of broken-down diners. Still, Ethan had managed to find one at the city limits. He shifted on his side of the booth, the red plastic fabric of the seat fraying underneath him. "Do you think the neighbors are lying about not having heard the gunshot?"

Annie took another bite of her almost-finished breakfast

sandwich, chewing over her thoughts. She swallowed. "I think they're lying about a large number of things, for a wide variety of reasons, none of them having to do— linearly— with why Mr. Markin is dead."

"I hate when you do that," he made a hand motion in the air. "The talking in circles thing."

"It makes sense to me," Annie smiled at him. "Maybe one day you'll just have to learn my pattern, and then you'll know exactly what I'm saying."

"I keep hoping," Ethan agreed. "You *could* just tell me who you suspect."

Annie shook her head. "You're an official officer of the law. Suspicions aren't facts. I can't, in good conscience, tell you who I suspect until I have the facts to back it up. It would be akin to declaring someone guilty without a trial."

"Did you get more facts today?"

"The most," Annie assured him. "There's still more to do, though."

"There always is," Ethan answered.

"We're ready for individual interviews."

"You've sufficiently riled them up?"

"I believe so," Annie agreed.

"Then it's time."

"It's time."

When the plates were cleaned and the diner had nothing left to offer, Annie and Ethan shared one car back to the motel they'd chosen to stay at, each of them on the uppermost floor. It was a lived-in kind of place— not at all up to the typical standards of a town like Watersborough— but it was what the FBI had been willing to spring for on a low-priority case. Paint peeled on the staircase banister, and there was a general odor of smoke about the rooms.

Annie stopped outside the door to her temporary home, key in hand. Beside her, Ethan did the same. The rooms they'd booked were side-by-side, which offered a constant invitation. It was one Annie was trying not to accept.

She looked at Ethan, her eyes addressing something unspoken.

"You need me, you know where I am," Ethan offered, not in the least bit offended. He knew Annie's ways— how she could be so strong in one moment, and so fragile in the next. He liked the unpredictability of the woman beside him, and he never took her preferences personally. He treated Annie like the rain, or the weather— as both a constant and something inevitable. Annie was a fact of life, if not a beautiful one.

For a second, something flashed across her face. Something Ethan hadn't seen in years. Then, as quickly as it came, the feeling left. "Tomorrow we do the one-on-one interviews," she said.

"We're closer, aren't we?" Ethan asked, and Annie couldn't help but believe he was talking about more than just the case.

"Goodnight," she said to her oldest friend, opening the door to her room and closing it softly behind her.

CHAPTER NINETEEN

OTTO

"THANK you for taking the time to meet with us," Detective Annie Hudson grinned at her subject. As the primary security guard on Aspen Lane, Otto was responsible for ensuring the wrong kind of people stayed outside the gates, and that the right kind of people were allowed in. He appeared to take pride in his job, judging by the way his blue uniform was crisply pressed and free from a single stain or wrinkle.

"It's no problem," Otto grunted, his mustache moving in time with his speech. He shifted a little, trying to make more space within the small, security guard's booth that perched at the end of Aspen Lane. It was tight, with three people inside the booth. Otto remained seated at the glass window, eyes always searching, while Annie and Ethan remained standing.

"We'll need you to confirm some events from the evening Mr. Markin was killed," Ethan added, exchanging a quick glance with Annie. His pen was perched over his clipboard, prepared to record the results of her line of questioning.

"You told the police no one came in or out that evening. Is that still correct?"

Otto nodded, agreeing to her point. "Didn't see a single

car. Not one visitor. It was a Sunday night. Sundays are usually quiet."

"Do you have evidence of that fact? A security camera tape or something similar."

"No camera," Otto answered. "But we keep a sign-in sheet for guests." Otto pulled a three-ring binder off the desk in front of him. He opened it, revealing pages of hand-written lists. He flipped to the date in question, showing Annie the empty ledger.

"Empty," Annie agreed.

Otto shut the binder, pausing for a moment as if deciding whether to say something. "The gate company keeps a record too, of the openings and closings. You can call them."

"We will," Ethan answered. "The FBI can subpoena the records."

"Excellent," Annie agreed. She moved toward the flat, built-in desk that took up half the space in Otto's tiny booth, perching on the edge of it like a cat on a window. Otto bristled at the imposition, but if he minded much, thought better of saying anything.

"We have multiple mysteries to solve here, Otto. And I think your help is key."

"My help?" Otto asked, concerned.

"Yes," Annie continued. "There's the mystery, of course, of who killed Mr. Markin. Given that no one entered or exited, it must be a resident of the street. Then we have the mystery of the robbery at Mr. Markin's house, which occurred just one week prior. Finally, we have the mystery... of me."

"You?"

"Me," Annie repeated. "I was hired by an anonymous source. A tip and some cash is all that led me here. Why would the person who hired me not simply reveal themselves?"

"I don't know," Otto shrugged. "Guess they had a reason."

"Guess so," Annie chirped, continuing as if they were

discussing the weather. "I'd like to take you back to one week ago, on the day Mr. Markin's house was robbed. Was this another day on which Aspen Lane was not subject to visitors?"

Otto shook his head, annoyed. "The opposite," he said, brows furrowed. "Had more visitors than I could stand."

"Why's that?"

"The boys in the newest house. Jared and the brothers. They like to throw parties. Can't stop them, apparently, as they're within their rights to do so. But the neighborhood hates it."

"And so do you," Annie confirmed.

Otto leaned back in his chair, uncomfortable with the way this female detective drew attention to what typically remained unspoken. "Anybody would," he answered, his tone defensive. "Checking in car after car. They fill up the street parking. The noise alone is enough to drive a man crazy. Just want some peace is all. This is supposed to be a peaceful neighborhood."

"Is peace something you're looking for?" Annie asked. When Otto didn't answer, she pointed at a stack of books on the end of the desk. There were so many tomes filling the space that Otto's tiny booth resembled a library. "I read too," she continued. "To find my peace."

"It's not that I mind doing the job," Otto answered, evasive. "Just didn't sign up to be dealing with a mob every time they have a party."

"I understand," Annie said sympathetically. "And how long have you had this job, at Aspen Lane, specifically?"

"Less than a year," Otto answered.

"Wonderful," Annie smiled. "Now, back to the day of the robbery. Did you notice anything strange? Any guests you think might have been the kind of person who would target Mr. Markin's home?"

"They all look like hoodlums," Mr. Markin shrugged.

"Could've been anyone. They were wearing swimsuits, so I figured the boys were throwing a pool party this time around. Didn't see a car make a break for it. I didn't even know anything unusual had happened until the police showed up."

"Of course," Annie said. "That's all we needed. Thank you, for your time," she stood, brushing off her pants like she'd just finished a hard day's work.

"That's it?" Otto muttered, surprised. "You don't have anything else to ask?"

"That's it," Annie smiled at him. "Pretty painless."

"Thank you," Ethan reached for Otto's hand, shaking it in a firm grip. "We'll be in touch."

With that, the two detectives exited Otto's booth, letting the glass doors slide shut behind them. He watched as they headed back toward the neighborhood, wondering how his job had suddenly become so complicated.

He stretched his arms upward for a moment, glad to be alone in his booth once again. He grabbed a book from his stack of paperbacks in the corner, the spine cracking as he opened the cover. He looked like a bird in a cage, perfectly happy now that his habitat was no longer under threat.

CHAPTER TWENTY

KRYSTAL

EVEN THOUGH SHE was expecting her visitors, the congenial ringing of the doorbell made Krystal's skin prickle. Through the sheer drapes that covered the living room window, she could just make out the rough outlines of two figures. As she approached the door, Krystal took a deep breath. All she needed to do was to be calm. This was the same as selling a tarot card reading to a skeptical client. She was selling her story, and she needed the detectives to buy it, hook, line, and sinker. Krystal was nothing if not persuasive. Her charm was her secret weapon. It was how she'd managed to rise to the top of this exclusive enclave after leaving Los Angeles with nothing but a broken-down van and ten dollars to her name.

"Come on in," Krystal beamed, opening the door to reveal Annie and Ethan. "Tea's just brewing."

She ushered them through the foyer and into the living room, where the table sat ready. Krystal had laid out a celestial tea set, stars and moons dotting the edges of the china.

"I use it for tea leaf readings sometimes," Krystal gushed about the set. "I could read yours if you're interested—"

"No time today, unfortunately," Annie answered, not a

hint of dissatisfaction in her pleasant tone. "But that's a kind offer. Maybe we'll visit you again if I can't solve the case and the FBI needs a psychic consultant."

Ethan bit his tongue. It was important to let Annie play with her subjects, the way a cat batted at a mouse before ending the charade with a bloodbath. Still, Ethan hated to allow anyone to entertain the idea that the FBI needed psychics.

"That would be wonderful!" Krystal exclaimed, pulling a tea kettle off the stove. "I've wanted to do some consulting. I'm so busy, what with the business thriving. But for something as important as helping the FBI, I could absolutely make the time—"

"How *kind* of you..." Ethan started to snarl before Annie kicked him under the table. He grabbed his teacup with both hands, making it look even smaller in his enormous grip.

"This will be brief," Annie continued, allowing Krystal to pour from the kettle into her cup. "I just had a couple of follow-up questions."

"Of course," Krystal nodded solemnly. "I've like, totally, known all along this would be a difficult case. From the cards," she clarified, pointing at a deck of Tarot cards sitting on the bookshelf. "When Mr. Markin was alive, they showed that someone close to him couldn't be trusted. A 'frenemy' was what I told him. Like a mean girl in high school! Someone around him was pretending to be his protector, but in reality, they were out to get him. He didn't believe me, of course." Krystal sipped her tea, eyes lowered.

"Is that because he wasn't the type of man to believe in psychics?" Annie prodded.

"No, it was more—" Krystal paused, trying to find the words to describe her old friend. "He believed the best in everyone. He couldn't wrap his head around the idea someone he knew might be planning to betray him. It just didn't fit with his view of the world. He chose to see people for their potential, not for their flaws."

"Interesting," Annie nodded, appreciating the confirmation of what she also had come to learn about Mr. Markin. "I'd like to ask you a few questions about your business if you don't mind."

"Anything you like," Krystal slid her hands under the table like they might give her away. "I'm an open book."

"We read the special feature on you in Watersborough magazine. The lifestyle edition." Annie reached into her briefcase, extracting a glossy copy of the local publication. She opened it, flipping to the centerfold. There, a photo of Krystal took up an entire page. In the picture, Krystal was lying on a pillow, a feather in her hair, tarot cards spread in front of her. "You're something of a local celebrity."

"I wouldn't say that," Krystal waved her away, but the smile tugging at her lips said she enjoyed the characterization. "I do what I can to help the community."

"It says here you're something of an entrepreneur, too," Annie read from the article. "You told the reporter you were planning on launching a full line of branded products. Krystal's Tarot Cards. Krystal's Incense. Krystal's candles."

"I'm a clever businesswoman," Krystal's tone suddenly shifted, alerting Annie to the fact that she had taken the correct trail. "Good business owners are always thinking about ways to diversify their product line."

"It sounds amazing," Annie agreed. "Do you have any samples to show us?"

A silence lingered in the air. "Samples?" Krystal asked, dumbfounded. "Of— of the products?"

"Yes," Annie smiled at her, always pleasant. "The candles. The tarot decks. I'd love to leave with something of a souvenir. What do you think, Ethan?" She turned to her partner, completely serious and rather congenial. "Wouldn't you love to leave Watersborough with your own Krystal-branded candle?"

"Oh sure," Ethan nodded gravely. "Would give me something to remember this wonderful experience by. Huge fan of psychics, by the way."

"I—" Krystal stuttered, unsure whether or not their flattery was genuine. Finally, she decided to take it as such. "I don't have any samples at the moment. The team is still working on the branding." She flipped her hair, recovering the veneer of her sparkle. "I need the logos to be consistent and it's *so* hard to find good designers these days."

"Understood," Annie answered. "We'll have to try again when you're ready to launch, then. You'll let us know?"

"Of course," Krystal agreed.

"Just out of curiosity," Annie leaned in. "How did you build this brand up from nothing? I mean, you're one of the top psychics on the East Coast, but you're a California transplant. It seems like you just arrived on the scene and— bam. Instant success."

"It helps to have a gift," Krystal smiled at her. "But it's also knowing how to run a business. How to find the right people. Being a female entrepreneur is an honor and a responsibility."

"It says here," Annie flipped through her documents. "You didn't have quite as much success in Los Angeles. It looks like you declared bankruptcy— one, two—" Annie counted on the page, "— three times— before leaving California entirely. Is that correct?"

"It's an expensive place to live," Krystal conceded. "Trial and error is key when you're an entrepreneur. It took me time to learn how to think of my gift not just as an act of service, but as a business. By the time I came to Watersborough, I'd learned a lot."

"Like how to avoid debt repayment?" Annie moved in for the kill. "It says in these court filings you had no fewer than ten private lenders that issued personal loans to you. When you filed for chapter eleven, they lost the opportunity to recoup their money."

"Those were friends and business partners," Krystal huffed. "When a motivated man takes a loan and it doesn't work he's a founder and CEO, but when I do it, suddenly it's an issue! I found seed money, the business failed, and I did what was necessary to start fresh. Investors know the risks."

"You're quite good at finding wealthy investors."

"Is that a crime?" Krystal bristled.

"No," Annie conceded. "Just a fascinating ability," she paused. "How *do* you do it?"

Krystal flushed. She hated being seen like this. Here in Watersborough, she'd had the chance to start over— to be known not as a grifter, but as an asset to the community. And now, this detective was threatening to ruin it all.

The truth was, Krystal did have a gift. Not just for reading the future, but for reading people. With each potential investor, she was able to find the tactic most suited to their individual weak points. An older man with no family might come to think of her as a granddaughter, and suddenly— he was investing in her business. A middle-aged man with a wife and kids might view her as an exciting escape from his life. She never crossed the line into allowing physical contact, of course— at least, not much of it. But she knew how to make a man so curious about the idea of sleeping with her that it drove him wild. With female investors, the key was often playing the "supporting young women" card. Whatever the strategy, Krystal was able to find a rich person's weak points and exploit them.

The irony was that Krystal wasn't lying about being psychic. She had made hundreds, maybe even thousands of accurate predictions. Krystal was a moderately capable psychic with some true talent. No, the place where Krystal went wrong was that she lied about where the money went. She borrowed from the business account frequently, because she liked the finer things in life. Expensive clothes. Nice cars. Top-of-the-line apartments. And sometimes, in LA, private table service at the finest clubs.

"I know people," Krystal confessed, unable to stop a little bit of shame from coloring the edge of her voice. "It's not illegal, to know people."

"I can't argue with that," Annie looked straight into Krystal's eyes, almost sorry to have solved the puzzle of her person so easily. "And based on what you've told me, it seems you knew Mr. Markin very well."

Krystal's silence told Annie everything she needed to know.

Annie stood, smoothing out her pants. Ethan followed, scooting his chair back. "Thank you so much for your time," Annie said, making her way to the front door. Krystal leaped from the table, opening the door for them, eager to see her guests out.

"If you have any more questions, it's no problem," Krystal forced a fake smile onto her face. She opened the door, allowing Annie and Ethan to exit onto the front steps. As they headed for the curb, Annie called over her shoulder:

"Let us know when we can buy some of those branded candles."

Krystal nodded, but deep down, she knew: she was utterly, completely, royally—*fucked*.

CHAPTER TWENTY-ONE

JARED

"WE DON'T HAVE to talk to you again," Edmonte scoffed. Jared watched as his brother stretched his legs long over a striped lawn chair. They were sitting by the pool in the backyard, across from Detectives Annie and Ethan. "Why should we help you? We'd be better off getting a lawyer."

"That's true," the female detective agreed, her smile unchanged. "Although, that would be an unusual move, considering we're no threat to you."

"This is just another line of questioning," her partner, Ethan added. "You're under no obligation to participate."

"We come in the interest of a personal favor," Annie said.

"Well I *personally* don't feel very generous," Edmonte said, adjusting his sunglasses. Jared hated when his brother took on this caricature of a personality. Edmonte liked to pretend their success made them more special than other people, but Jared knew the truth: they were a joke on the internet, making money performing for strangers who were waiting with glee for the day Jared seriously hurt himself. The stunts Jared performed were dangerous, and viewers only tuned in for the spectacle of it all. When Jared ultimately ended up in a coma, or full body cast, or maybe worse, it would become a headline on a gossip website, and that would be it. The fans would mourn publicly in a strange performance of grief, and then move on. And his brothers? They would find something else to do. Without him.

"*Edmonte,* be nice," Jared's youngest brother, Marcus, prodded. He was nervous, bouncing up and down as he arranged snacks on the table. Marcus knew how Edmonte could get.

"Shouldn't you be getting us more drinks?" Edmonte snarled at his brother. Marcus shirked, moving back toward the kitchen in a defeated slouch. Jared watched his younger brother's body language with a pain in his chest. This business had ruined them. Ruined every single one of them before they'd even really gotten a start in life.

"What's all this for?" The female detective pointed behind them, appearing genuinely curious. On the lawn sat a soft mat and an enormous canon, big enough to fit a human inside. A helmet and jumpsuit with an American flag pattern hung on a clothing rack beside the canon, a light-kit set up to run on extension cords.

"They're launching me from a canon," Jared heard himself say. His voice sounded glum and far away. He'd been sober for a whopping eight hours, and the feeling was crushing. A familiar pressure sat on his chest. He'd need a fix before this next stunt.

"Jared," Edmonte looked a little surprised, maybe even betrayed. "We're not— that's—" he turned to Annie as if he needed to defend himself. "Jared's *choosing* to get launched from the canon. We're paying homage to the original bad boy, Evil Knievel. It's a nostalgic piece, channeling the simplicity of times gone by. We think it's going to break the internet. It was Jared's idea and he's the driving creative force."

"It looks that way," Annie nodded at Jared, who glanced up at her. He hadn't noticed he had his head in his hands. He applied pressure to the space between his eyebrows, trying to make the pounding stop.

"Edmonte," Jared said, once again feeling as if his body weren't his own. "Go help Marcus with the craft services before the crew gets here."

Edmonte's mouth dropped open, shocked to be given a direct order. Jared didn't wait for him to verbalize his protest. "Now," he said. And that was it. Edmonte stood as if in a dream, and without another word— crossed the lawn and dismissed himself from the gathering. His figure disappeared into the sliding doors that led into the kitchen, the glass rattling with a resounding bang as they shut behind him.

Jared was alone with the two detectives. He shifted in his chair, ready to do whatever was necessary to make the pain stop.

"I know why you're here," Jared said.

"And why's that?" Annie asked.

"You know it was me who broke into Mr. Markin's house."

"The vanity in the bathroom," Annie said. "There's a space behind the wall. An excellent place to hide something."

Jared nodded. She'd noticed the same thing he had the night he'd stashed his drugs at Mr. Markin's house.

"Do you want to tell us what happened?" Annie's voice pierced Jared's headache, a clarion call. It was now or never. He could either tell the truth, and be the man Mr. Markin believed he could be, or he could hide.

"He was my friend," Jared said, unable to ignore the way his voice shook. "Mr. Markin was— maybe— my only real friend." Suddenly, Jared's breathing became shallow. His eyes burned. He wouldn't cry in front of these detectives. It would be too embarrassing. "He was helping me. I have a problem. To do these videos, it's not easy..."

"Of course not," Annie said, putting a hand on Jared's knee as if she cared about him. Jared knew it was probably just her way of extracting information, but the gesture still meant something. So few people worried about him, it was nice to feel cared for.

"It started after an injury," Jared told her. "They gave me painkillers. The problem is I get hurt a lot, and now I want them even when I'm fine," he paused, wishing he could make these two strangers understand how he'd gotten here. "The thing you have to understand is we come from nothing. My parents, they were always high. Our house growing up, it wasn't like this..." he motioned around the yard. "We'd come home and the door would be unlocked and they'd both be passed out. No dinner. No help with homework. Nobody really cared what happened to me. So when I was a teenager I did stupid stuff and put it on the internet. I did dangerous shit maybe because I was testing everyone, or—" The truth seemed to leak out of Jared against his will. "Or maybe because I didn't totally want to be here anymore and I did these things to make it stop—"

Jared didn't know if he was making any sense. His words came out in a tangle, but in his mind, the images were clear. His life so far flashed before him in a twisted knot of pictures and feelings. Thirteen-year-old Jared, recording himself skateboarding in a leap across two rooftops. That had been his first stunt, and he'd never forgotten the way he'd felt complete peace in the midst of danger. Sixteen-year-old Jared, launching a motorcycle off a homemade ramp. The way he felt when he was suspended in the air, eerily calm about the prospect of death.

"Doing the stunts made me feel more alive, but also closer to death," Jared continued. "I honestly think I put them on the internet hoping someone would see how dangerous it was and would stop me before I got hurt. Like, maybe a teacher would tell my parents and they would care all of a sudden and tell me not to do it anymore. Or maybe they'd act like everyone else's parents and ground me. But that didn't happen," he wiped his nose with the back of his sleeve. "Instead, we just made money. And more money. And all of a sudden, we had more money than we knew what to do with, and now we're here, living this life. But it's all because of the videos. I can't stop making them, or the money stops. And if the money stops, my brothers— they won't be able to do anything else. This is our only work experience. We don't have degrees or training. This is it. This is what we do."

Jared shivered. He'd never told anyone besides Mr. Markin this story before, and it felt cathartic to get it off his chest. It was like sucking out the poison from a snakebite.

"Mr. Markin knew all of this?" Annie asked, patient.

"He knew everything. He was helping me try to change it. Talking to me about college and different careers I could do. But he said first I needed to get clean. He believed in me," Jared added, his voice trembling. "We got to talking one day in the cul-de-sac. Then we talked again the next day. And the day after that. We're both home a lot because he's retired. And then we started talking *every* day, and he invited me to come over for breakfast. It just kind of grew from there. He tried to help me. I was actually sober for three weeks because of Mr. Markin, which is the longest I've ever lasted. But then — I came to his house one morning, and I had the drugs on me. He told me over breakfast how proud he was of me—"

Jared remembered it with the kind of clarity that comes from a life moment that changes everything. He'd been sitting at Mr. Markin's kitchen table, sharing the scrambled eggs and bacon that Mr. Markin always offered. They'd each had a cup of coffee in front of them, and Jared had been thinking this is how his friends growing up must have felt when they sat with their own families. It was something he'd never had.

As they usually did, Mr. Markin and Jared had discussed the various happenings of their individual days. Mr. Markin would tell Jared about his volunteer work with the Key Club, and Jared would tell Mr. Markin about his next death-defying stunt. "I don't understand it," Mr. Markin would tell him. "Just do me a favor and wear a helmet." This was their personal joke. Mr. Markin would tell Jared to wear a helmet no matter what he was doing. "I'm going to free dive in an underwater cave," Jared would say. Mr. Markin would answer, "Don't forget to wear a helmet."

That morning, like any other, Mr. Markin claimed he didn't understand Jared's latest stunt— walking across hot coals barefoot— but once again, he advised that Jared "wear a helmet."

It was then that Jared had decided to tell a small lie. He wasn't sure why he did it, except that Mr. Markin had been so nice to him, and he worried, perhaps, it would stop if he didn't reach some kind of milestone. "I called the recovery place you gave me the pamphlet for," Jared had said, pushing his eggs around his plate. "I'm not saying I'm going. Just that I'm thinking about it." Jared had tried to keep his voice casual. He was worried Mr. Markin would try to push him into something, and Jared hated being pushed into things.

"Interesting," Mr. Markin said casually, as if he knew what Jared was thinking and didn't wish to give him any reason to rebel. Mr. Markin had stood and walked across the kitchen to get the coffee creamer, then said— casually, as if he were commenting on the weather—

"You know I'm proud of you, son."

The word "proud" had taken Jared by surprise. No one— *no one*— had ever been proud of him. He wasn't a person worth being proud of. Guilt had flooded Jared's veins. Mr. Markin didn't know that at that exact moment, Jared had drugs on him in a small plastic bag, tucked away in a back pocket. In fact, Jared was a little bit high right then, but was so high-functioning he was sure Mr. Markin couldn't tell.

Jared changed the topic back to his video stunt, and then looked for the perfect moment to exit. He excused himself to go to the bathroom. Once there, he searched the small space for a spot to hide the drugs, panicked that— if they happened to fall out of his pocket, or appeared by some chance in Mr. Markin's line of view— the man he so admired would suddenly want nothing to do with him.

"I panicked," Jared said aloud, eyes cast at the ground beneath his feet. "I wasn't thinking straight. I worried the drugs would fall out of my pocket, or that he'd find out somehow. It didn't make sense. I should've just kept them on me and he would have never known. But I don't always think clearly, when I'm high, and I didn't want him to see."

"I understand," Annie said. "So you hid them behind the vanity?"

Jared nodded. "That space? I just stuck them back there and wedged them between the wall and the back of the sink." Jared sighed, the memory of what he'd done hanging heavy in the air. "I was high right there, sitting and having breakfast with him," Jared's voice came out as a whisper. "And he didn't even know."

"I'm sure he knew," Annie corrected him. Jared stared at her, surprised. "Mr. Markin was an astute man. I'm sure he knew you were high and chose to care about you anyway."

The idea rocked Jared to his core. He had never considered that he'd overestimated his ability to hide his intoxication, while simultaneously underestimating Mr. Markin's ability to love him past it.

"But the robbery?" Ethan couldn't help but ask, feeling rather shocked at the entire exchange. "You broke into his house later? Why?"

"To retrieve the drugs," Annie answered on Jared's behalf. "You were worried Mr. Markin would find them."

"Yes," Jared cringed. "Once I got home I started sobering up and realized how stupid it was to leave them there. Plus, I needed another fix. Needed it bad. So I broke into his house when I knew he'd be gone at the Key Club and my brothers were throwing a pool party. But then I realized it would look really strange that nothing was stolen."

"So you took the vase," Annie concluded.

"I just grabbed it because it was in the bathroom. It kind of looked expensive, but I'm not great at telling what costs a lot. I just thought it looked fancy and Mr. Markin's rich, so probably everything in his house is worth something."

"Thieves don't usually rob a house and leave with just a vase worth a few hundred bucks," Ethan said.

"They would where I'm from," Jared shrugged. "A few hundred dollars is a lot." Jared paused, crossing his arms in front of him as if he were hugging himself. "I wish I had gotten to tell him it was me. I was planning on telling him one day. I was gonna tell him the whole story, but only after I really got clean. So I could say I'd done this bad thing, but I'd made up for it by being the man he believed I could be. He always said that to me. That he believed I could be a great man."

Jared couldn't help it now. The tears broke loose from their prison, dripping down his face in unwilling lines. He didn't even try to wipe them away.

"I think, just now, you've succeeded in that," Annie smiled at him. “And what about the lawn furniture in Reggie and Janis’s backyard? Did you rearrange that the day of the robbery?”

“No,” Jared shrugged. “I don’t know anything about that. But I know Janis was home because I saw her watering plants in the front yard when I was waiting for the right moment to go from my house to Mr. Markin’s house. I had to wait for her to go inside to make my move. I don’t know why she would lie about being gone,” he added.

“I can only guess,” Annie smiled.

"What's gonna happen now? Am I going to prison?" Jared asked, almost hopeful. Maybe prison would separate him from his vices long enough that he could start again, even at rock bottom.

"No," Annie assured him. "Rehab, probably, but not prison. Could you do me another favor? It will help you, as well."

Jared nodded.

"Don't share this story with anyone just yet," Annie continued. "I want to bring Mr. Markin the justice he deserves by finding the person who killed him. And if you tell anyone what happened, it might tip my hand."

"I won't say anything," Jared answered, surprised at her request. The Detectives stood, heading for the glass doors.

"Annie?" Jared called out behind them. Annie and Ethan stopped and turned. Jared took a breath. He thought about Mr. Markin and the way he had made Jared feel at home. The way they'd laughed in their conversations at the end of the cul-de-sac. The way he'd looked forward to sitting in Mr. Markin's kitchen, the old cabinets and bad wallpaper all fond memories of a place where he'd felt he belonged. He thought about the way Mr. Markin had always called him "son," without ever knowing what it had meant to him. That every time he heard the word drop from Mr. Markin's mouth, he'd wanted to perform his stunts even less because— for the first time— Jared felt he had someone in his life who would be worried about him if he was hurt. Mr. Markin had given him both a person he hated to disappoint, and a person he wanted to make proud. Mr. Markin had given him a parent.

"Whoever killed Mr. Markin deserves what they get. Promise you'll catch them?"

Annie's eyes crinkled, emotion in the crow's feet that formed there. It was as if she understood what this meant to Jared. It was as if she felt his pain as her own— like it was familiar to her. "I promise you," she answered, "I will."

CHAPTER TWENTY-TWO

JANIS

JANIS PREFERRED to let Reggie do the talking. She sat at their kitchen table, examining the pattern in the paisley tablecloth she'd laid down only yesterday. Next to her, Reggie was staring down their two guests: Detectives Annie and Ethan.

"We hardly knew him, that's the truth," Reggie said, explaining their seemingly distant connection to Mr. Markin. "We're always on the move because of the kids. Not much time to get to know the neighbors. You should try Frank. He was close to the man. They had the family military connection, I believe—"

"We'll absolutely follow that lead, thank you," Annie agreed. "You've been very helpful. We apologize we had to inconvenience you again like this."

"It's fine," Reggie waved a hand and checked his watch. "Wish we could do more to help but it is what it is."

"Actually," Annie laid her trap, her voice inviting. "Ethan wanted to run a few things by you regarding the FBI's strategy."

"I did?" Ethan asked, surprised.

"Yes," Annie continued, turning back to Reggie. "We heard

you're one of the best investors in town. Ethan's working on a case that involves financial crimes. He'd love a word with you—"

"— in the other room," Ethan caught her drift. "It's sensitive stuff. I shouldn't even be sharing outside of the FBI."

"I wouldn't mind lending an ear," Reggie puffed out his chest and stood up from the table, motioning for Ethan to follow. "I've got a Whiskey we can crack open in my office. Ladies, you know where to find us."

Ethan followed Reggie out of the kitchen, shooting a meaningful glance over his shoulder at Annie. Only for her sake would he take this bullet.

Annie turned to Janis, finally alone with the true subject of her investigation this afternoon. "We don't have much time, so I apologize in advance that I won't be able to apply my usual tact."

"I'm used to people being rather blunt," Janis answered, her voice resigned. She had expected this.

"The murder. The robbery. The letter. You are my solution to two of those mysteries," Annie stated simply. "The night Mr. Markin was killed, you—"

"I know. I know what you're going to say."

"Then you know what you have to do," Annie pushed.

Janis was statue-like, her stoic limbs immobilized for a moment. Then, she buried her face in her hands. The tears welled even as she tried to stop them, dropping onto that tablecloth like a confession.

"It will ruin me," she said. Then, she looked out the window. In the front yard, her two boys played catch, tossing a baseball back and forth. "It will ruin *them.*"

"Really?" Annie laughed. The reaction was inappropriate, but not unwarranted. "I'm sorry, it's just— you don't think this, the dynamic between you and your husband, isn't already ruining them?" She leaned in, serious. "Do you want them to move out of this home one day and find a wife they can treat just the way he's treated you? As someone who is invisible? Or do you want them to leave and go into the world knowing they can have the courage to be the truest version of themselves because that's what their Mom did? Look at how much you have to teach them." Annie paused, scanning the face of the woman in front of her. "They don't even *know* you right now. They know a version of you, yes, but not the real you, unfiltered and honest. Imagine how much courage you could give them, especially on the off chance they take after you."

The shadow of an unfamiliar emotion fell across Janis's face. Rage spread into the fine lines on her forehead, its tendrils animating every small muscle in her countenance. "You're using my *children.* How *dare* you!" She stood, pushing her chair out with force. She made her way to the sink, turning on the water and letting it run over the dishes. She grabbed a plate as she spoke. "You enter *my* home and try to tell me how to parent!" Janis scrubbed furiously, but it brought no relief.

"Just because I have a motive in making my argument, doesn't mean I'm not correct."

Janis dropped the plate, allowing it to make a clanging sound as it fell into the sink. She turned, leaning her back against the counter. The rage left her body as quickly as it had come, and suddenly she deflated, allowing defeat to wash over her in waves.

"What gave us away?"

"That's a beautiful bowl," Annie answered, nodding at a piece of pottery positioned on the kitchen island. It was hand-made, pieces of shattered glass carefully arranged within the rust-colored clay. The bowl perched in a place of prestige, displaying apples ripe for the taking. "It was clearly made with care."

"That's all it took?" Janis wondered.

"The line of sight," Annie added. "The fact you lied about

being away from home the day of the robbery when the lawn furniture was moved around. And maybe, also— just the way you look at each other. It was quite evident at the neighborhood meeting."

"You pay attention. Everyone else around here is so busy thinking about themselves. It made me feel safe, not being seen."

"Understandable."

"Then you also know who killed Mr. Markin—"

"I have a suspicion I believe is correct," Annie answered. "But there are evidentiary loose ends to tie up. I can't make a case on a hunch. I need facts. The murder weapon remains a problem. And you'll need to cooperate eventually, of course."

"How much time can you give me?" Janis's eyes welled up again, but this time, no tears fell. She was beyond tears. Now, all that was left was the business of it.

"A couple of days," Annie answered. "I believe, at that point, I'll have the evidence necessary to make an arrest."

"And you'll have to share the whole story, I suppose. Not just a piece of it."

"I don't believe it will make sense, otherwise," Annie confirmed.

"That's alright," Janis wiped her nose on her sleeve, almost relieved the facade was done. "It's been a long time coming."

"I'll show myself out," Annie said, making her way toward the front door. She paused before exiting. "Janis?"

"Yes?"

"You did the right thing. It was the wrong thing, in so many ways, but given the circumstances, it took quite a lot of courage. And, if it means anything," Annie looked away, wishing she could escape her own mind. "This is disappointing for me too."

"How so?" Janis asked, surprised.

"The envelope. The way you wrote the summons," Annie confessed. "It was personal, for me."

Janis's brow furrowed as she wondered what "personal" could possibly mean. But before Janis could seek answers, Annie called down the hallway. "Got a call! Time to move!"

As if by magic, Ethan emerged from the study, looking exhausted. Reggie appeared behind him, still offering financial tips.

"And don't forget about the black market, that's the place to look. All over the dark web," Reggie continued over Ethan's assurances.

"Super helpful," Ethan said as he darted toward the front door. He noticed Janis, still leaning against the sink, her face flushed. Before he could ask any questions. Annie opened the front door and ushered him out.

"We'll be in touch," she said only to Janis before letting the door close softly behind her.

Janis turned back toward the dishes in the sink, looking at them with a strange feeling of relief. They were a part of the life she was about to lose. She had dreaded this moment, but now that it had arrived, she was almost glad to have the chance to burn everything down and start again.

She stared at Reggie like she was seeing him for the first time.

"Can you finish the dishes? I need to go for a walk," she told him. Reggie's mouth dropped open, but before he could say a word, Janis had left, the back door clanging shut behind her.

CHAPTER TWENTY-THREE

SHEILA

IT WAS dark in Sheila's pottery studio. She'd made sure to keep the outside lights off, as she always did when it was this kind of evening. The sconces in the front yard failed to illuminate the house's exterior, ensuring the narrow path that led to the studio's side entrance remained shrouded in shadow.

Sheila knew Melissa was at the University, leading a faculty meeting, but still, she took every precaution to hide her activities on the off chance her wife came home early. Over time and many road bumps in their relationship, Sheila had learned to see Melissa's unpredictable schedule as a blessing. It allowed Melissa to feel empowered by the exterior employment she used to validate her existence, and it gave Sheila time to meet her own needs.

Sheila sat on the couch, waiting, two wine glasses and an uncorked bottle of pinot noir on the hand-crafted table beside her. The object of her affection was about to arrive, and it wasn't Melissa. At least, not anymore.

Just then, the side door creaked open. A familiar figure emerged from the shadows, wrapping a jacket around her narrow shoulders.

Janis.

Every time Sheila saw Janis, it still felt like the first time. When they'd moved to Aspen Lane, Sheila and Melissa had done the obligatory "meeting of the neighbors" tour. Right away, Sheila had seen something magnetic in Janis. Janis barely spoke and let her husband, Reggie, do most of the connecting on the first day they'd shown up at their neighbor's door. Of course, Melissa and Reggie had encountered each other with a frosty first meeting. Sheila remembered the way Melissa had said to Reggie, "This is my *wife*, but it looks like you have a problem with that?"

"No problem here," Reggie had answered. "Except with people being pushy about their... activities."

"What's that supposed to mean?" Melissa had countered.

"Nothing except that you should just do what you do, not make a scene about it."

A fight immediately ensued, souring the relationship for months to come. But the fight was restricted to Melissa and Reggie. While they argued with one another, Sheila and Janis had locked eyes, some kind of immediate connection brewing, as unexplainable as it was assured. They both knew what it was like to be married to an overpowering spouse. They both knew how it felt to be invisible beneath the gaze of the one who's supposed to love you most. They had more in common than they did separating them.

Over time, they'd gotten to know one another with simple gifts. Janis had stopped by with some cookies. Sheila found excuses to visit Janis with offerings of pottery, especially when she knew Reggie wouldn't be home. And then one day, Sheila had invited Janis to come to the pottery studio for a lesson in making art, and, well— they'd made more than that.

"What's wrong?" Sheila asked, staring at Janis in the doorway. She could tell Janis wasn't her usual self by the way she avoided eye contact. Sheila's heart quickened. Maybe their affair was about to end. It had been too good to be true anyway. For the first time since moving overseas, Sheila had been happy.

"They know," Janis said, taking off her coat and sitting next to Sheila on the couch. "The detectives."

Sheila's first reaction was relief— Janis *wasn't* leaving her after all— followed by fear. "No," Sheila said, shaking her head. "They couldn't. Not unless," Sheila paused, a thought occurring to her. "You didn't tell them?"

"I didn't mean to. The female detective— Annie—figured it out. We don't have much time. She's going to tell everyone, and then the whole town will know. It's my fault," Janis's voice shook. "You said we should do nothing and sit tight, but I just couldn't."

"What did you do?" Sheila gasped.

"I just couldn't sleep knowing what I know. I had to do something."

Suddenly, Sheila understood. She let the information wash over her, trying to move from her heart to her head. They needed to be smart— logical. That was how Sheila operated, whereas Janis was all heart.

"It's alright," Sheila conceded, pulling Janis close to her. "You did what you felt was right." She brushed Janis's hair out of her face. "Now what?"

Janis paused, considering. "We have to tell them before the Detectives tell everyone else. Which means—"

"Yes?" Sheila's heart raced.

"We have to decide, about us. Are we in this one hundred percent, or not at all?"

"You know where I stand," Sheila answered. "It's you who isn't sure."

"It's the kids. But maybe also, just that I was afraid," Janis said. "But I'm not afraid anymore. We'll tell them both. And then there's no going back." She leaned in, kissing Sheila like it was the first time. "And after that, it's just you and me."

Sheila smiled. These were the words she'd been wanting

to hear since their affair had started months ago, and— while she felt immense guilt over the way they had arrived—hearing them aloud sent a wave of peace through her body. She didn't realize how badly she'd wanted this until it had finally happened.

"You and me," Sheila whispered, willing to do whatever was necessary to make that idea her reality.

"We'll tell them," Janis added. "It's time."

CHAPTER TWENTY-FOUR

FRANK

AN EVENING BREEZE wafted in through the open sliding doors at the edge of Frank and Lisa's sunken living room. Crickets chirped in the night air. Typically, their songs comforted Frank, serving as a sign no other sounds would interrupt his evening. If Frank could hear the crickets, all was right with the world. But tonight, Frank felt their chirps were a warning, issued in rhythmic blasts.

Beware. Beware. Beware.

Frank turned his attention to the two detectives sitting in front of him: Annie and Ethan. They were both smiling, as if they'd come to talk about the weather, or were here on holiday.

Frank risked a glance at his only family in the world— his wife Lisa and his son Malcolm— sitting respectively on his left and right side. They perched next to him on the couch, all three of them looking as if they'd been called to the principal's office.

"Did you know your basement window is broken?" Annie, the female detective, pointed out the sliding doors at a part of the home that jutted out into the backyard. There, the basement window was slightly ajar, its rusted frame fighting against the act of closure.

"We haven't had a chance to fix it," Frank said, bristling against her words like they were an accusation.

"You should fix it," Annie said, deadpan. "All kinds of pests can get in. It's very bad to leave it open like that. Outright dangerous."

Ethan cleared his throat, fully aware not everyone enjoyed Annie's unique rhythm in a conversation. "Thank you for meeting us so late," he said.

"It's no trouble at all," Lisa answered. Her tone suggested she was equally as nonplussed about the entire affair. She might as well have been at coffee with one of the women from her knitting club. But Frank knew exactly what was on his wife's mind: the missing gun in their cabinet, which they still had been unable to locate.

Frank had searched the house from top to bottom, and even painstakingly investigated his adult son's room when he was out, fearing that perhaps Malcolm had intended to use the gun on himself. Eventually, he'd asked Malcolm about the gun's whereabouts, and Malcolm had said he didn't know. Frank believed him. His son was a man of honor and always had been. He might be struggling now, but the only person Malcolm took his problems out on was himself.

"You must get tired of sitting in the same living room again and again," Lisa said to the detectives, her voice snapping Frank out of his revelry. "The houses were all constructed by the same builder," Lisa motioned around the living room. "They look quite similar."

"No," Annie smiled at her. "It's not boring at all. We've loved seeing how everyone's put their personal touches into place. Each one is different. Yours, well, it's—" she paused, looking for the right word, "— homey."

Beside her, the male detective— Agent Ethan Beckett, as Frank remembered from his various Google searches on the pair— shuffled a stack of papers in front of him. "We're here to ask for some clarification on a couple of points that weren't addressed during the group meeting."

"You couldn't make it?" Annie asked Malcolm, staring straight at him. "The group meeting," she added as if to clarify.

"I didn't know it was happening," Malcolm shrugged.

"We should've told him," Frank interjected, eager to place the blame where it belonged. "But the letter wasn't clear who you expected to attend. Malcolm recently moved back in with us after his work situation shifted."

"I was in Iraq," Malcolm cut Frank off, an edge to his voice. Frank could be overprotective of his son, only because he knew the obstacles Malcolm was facing. But at times, it made Malcolm feel infantilized. Frank knew as much and tried to keep from being overbearing, but Malcolm was his only child and he'd spent so long worrying about him in combat that he knew no other way to be. "I did multiple tours. Was there right up until the withdrawal," Malcolm added, a strange nostalgia in his eyes.

"And you moved back in with your parents to figure out your next steps?"

Malcolm nodded. "I don't know much besides the army. I've been through combat. Lived in the desert. Watched better men than me not make it out. And now that I'm leaving the army, I have to figure out what I want to be. It's like starting over."

"Any ideas?" Annie smiled at him.

"I'd like to live in the neighborhood to stay close to my parents," Malcolm told her. "But I'll probably never be able to afford it. I wish I could though, seeing as we were all apart from each other for a long time when I was deployed. I'd like to start a family. I like working with cars. Could see starting my own garage someday. Would need to adjust to the sound of engines backfiring," he paused, thinking out loud. "I think I am, though. It's getting better."

Nobody spoke, and Malcolm's face shifted as he realized he hadn't shared the most important part of his story.

"We try to keep the house quiet," Frank added, helping his son. "After all the combat, Malcolm *needs* quiet."

"PTSD," Malcolm said, shaking his head. "I don't like labels, but that's what they've told me I have. Don't like to think of it that way, though. I like to just say I've heard enough sounds to last me a lifetime and I need a little time to shake it off."

"I relate to that," Annie nodded. Frank noticed the way her hands tightened around the edge of her jacket. There was a look in her eyes like she was remembering something. For a moment, Frank felt that he could trust this woman to empathize with his son. Maybe she wasn't the enemy after all. Still, this wasn't a hunch on which he could barter Malcolm's future. "I relate to that more than you know." Her hands loosened, and she looked toward Malcolm with a curious glint in her eye. "The parties Jared and his brothers throw. Those must bother you?"

"Not too much," Malcolm said, a lie crossing his eyes. "I deal with it."

"We try to ask the neighbors to keep the noise down as much as possible," Frank added. "Not that anyone listens. They still throw their parties and build their pottery studios, the rest of us be damned."

"How can we help with Mr. Markin's case?" Lisa spoke, directing the conversation back to the salient points. Before the detective's arrival, the group had engaged in a family meeting, agreeing not to mention the gun. Frank— as a lawyer— had advised his wife and son to keep only to the relevant points, lest something they say accidentally cast new suspicion. It was always better to say less when it came to legal matters. He had momentarily forgotten his own rule, but Lisa had—thankfully— saved him.

"Yes," the female detective answered, pulling a photograph out of her briefcase. "We were wondering if you could shed some light on this event?"

Frank's throat tightened. The photograph had been taken six months earlier. In the image, Malcolm was front and center, surrounded by retired military veterans, their hats and clothing indicating they'd also served in the army. Mr. Markin was next to Malcolm his arm around him, like a son. There was a time Frank felt grateful Malcolm had someone to relate to— someone to share in his experience. Now, he felt the whole thing had been a huge mistake.

"Mr. Markin took me to his squadron reunion," Malcolm offered. "He was helping me deal with the— you know— trouble with sounds. He thought it would be useful if I went to speak with some other vets who were older than me and had moved on to have other experiences." He chewed on the corner of his cheek for a moment. "That's the hardest part about it, you know. This feeling that you did something big, that mattered, and now— it's hard to look ahead and believe there's a future for you."

"Of course," Annie encouraged. "And how did it go?"

"It was nice being around the guys," Malcolm answered. "I miss my team. Miss being a part of something. It was the same feeling there. These guys— they would die for each other. Some of them hadn't talked for years but it was like they picked up right where they left off."

"What about Mr. Markin?" Annie asked, leaning forward in her seat. "How did he handle the reunion? It must have been hard."

Despite his efforts not to show emotion, Frank felt his eyebrows arch in surprise at the question. Malcolm, too, seemed moved by the way Annie seemed to have read Mr. Markin's personality without ever meeting him.

"Funny you'd ask that," Malcolm answered. "It *was* tough for him. There'd been a dozen reunions before that one, and Mr. Markin had never been. He only went to this one because of me."

"Malcolm," Annie shifted in her seat, the tone in the room suddenly serious. "I hate to put this pressure on you because I know Mr. Markin was your friend. You most likely told each other things you swore not to share with anyone else. Is that right?"

"Yes," Malcolm confirmed calmly. "I did promise him that."

Frank's mouth dropped open. He knew Mr. Markin was helping his son past his trauma, but he had no idea there were secrets between them.

"The trouble is," Annie continued, "I have a hunch about who killed Mr. Markin. "And I can't be sure I'm right without confirming a suspicion I have regarding Mr. Markin's past. I'm afraid that *you* may be the only person alive today— besides the murderer, of course— who knows the truth about his past."

Malcolm took this in and Frank watched, remembering again that his son was a man of honor. Malcolm reached up, scratching the scruff of his beard. "I could break a promise if it meant bringing his killer to justice," he said. "But I'd need more specifics. To make sure I'm telling you the right thing."

"Fair enough," Annie agreed. She stood, suddenly pacing across the room, lost in a fever dream of her own making. "The thing I've learned about Mr. Markin is he was a person of ethics and morals. He helped others. He went out of his way to nurture and mentor. Right here in this very cul-de-sac, he changed lives for the better. But I asked myself— why would a person be so dedicated to doing the right thing? His community service surpasses any spiritual, moral, or religious calling. And then it hit me—" she stopped in her tracks as if the idea had donned on her once again, "—he was atoning. Atoning for something that happened in his youth." She sat, taking her place in her chair once again. "I called his squadron's reunion leader. They told me exactly what you did. That this was the first reunion Mr. Markin had attended. Do you know what tends to keep people away from a place they'd otherwise like to be?"

Malcolm nodded but allowed Annie to verbalize the answer anyway.

"Shame," Annie said. "Shame keeps people from going where they want to go and doing what they ought to do." She paused, locking eyes with Malcolm once again. "Mr. Markin was ashamed because of something that happened with his squadron, wasn't he?"

Frank watched his son for a reaction. At first, it seemed as if Malcolm wouldn't say anything at all, but then he let out a large exhale, and his shoulders slumped.

"He was," Malcolm said, his voice pained. "The thing you have to understand is that nobody knows what it's like out there until they're face-to-face with war. Everybody thinks they're 'gonna be a hero, but when the time comes and there's death all around, everything in you tells you to run—"

"It could happen to any of us," Annie confirmed.

"In Vietnam, Mr. Markin did a lot of good things. He helped with the medical unit. Was there for his team. But he was just a kid. He was younger than I was when I enlisted, and they got under enemy fire. It wasn't his whole squadron, thankfully— just a couple of guys. But the Viet Cong was on top of them, and Mr. Markin's guys were about to get captured, and he saw a way out. So—"

"So he took it?" Annie added.

Malcolm nodded. "He ran. Left them behind and ran as fast as he could. He regretted it the moment he got back to the rest of the squadron, because of no man left behind and everything. He told the rest of his squadron and they all went out together to find the two other guys, but it was too late— they'd been captured. Mr. Markin never found out what happened to them, but he figures they were killed."

"Did he stay in the army?"

"No, not after that," Malcolm answered. "He was able to get discharged. But the regret— it followed him. He told me he thought about what he'd done every day and he promised himself he'd live a better life. That any chance he got to help somebody, he would do it." Malcolm paused, looking up at the ceiling. "As far as I'm concerned, he kept that promise."

"It looks that way from where I'm sitting as well," Annie agreed. "And the reunion?"

"He told me he'd go to the reunion to prove to me that you can't let the past hold you back. He did it to be an example. We helped each other. We went together to be brothers in arms," Malcolm's eyes welled up and his cheeks flushed, but he held back the feeling. "His death— It's another big loss, for me."

Frank reeled. It struck him all of a sudden that he'd been living in the same home as his son— worrying over noises and sounds and Malcolm's comfort— but had never really seen this side of him at all. Frank reached out, putting an arm around Malcolm's shoulder.

"Have I told you today how proud I am of you?" He asked, forgetting anyone else was in the room.

"Only five times," Malcolm grinned at him.

"Let's make it six," Frank added. He turned to Annie, ready for the interview to conclude. "I'd love to wrap this up. Is there anything else?"

"No," Annie smiled, standing up and smoothing her pants back into place. "I can't thank you all enough. Ethan and I won't infringe anymore on your hospitality."

Her partner stood, reaching out to shake Malcolm's hand.

"Thank you for your service," he said, genuinely meaning it. "And for helping us here, today."

They turned to leave, but Annie paused at the door, turning around to face the family once again. "Oh," she tapped her forehead as if she'd forgotten something. "Silly me, there was one more thing. We were able to pull Malcolm's service history, and it stated he's a firearm champion."

Frank felt like the wind had been knocked out of him, but he tried not to let the emotion cross his face.

"Yes," Lisa answered, her voice sounding far away. "Our son won multiple medals for his service. That was one of them."

"Of course!" Annie exclaimed, her tone bright. "I was wondering... you don't keep any guns on the property, do you?"

There was a long pause where nobody said anything, and the air hung heavy in the room. It was Malcolm who broke the silence.

"Yes," he answered honestly. "I keep them all in the basement in a gun case. It's locked, and the ammo is always stored separately." He left it at that, and Frank was relieved that his son was an honorable man, but not a stupid one.

"I don't suppose I could see it?" Annie asked.

"The guns are out being serviced," Frank said, trying not to let his voice betray him.

"No trouble at all," Annie smiled. "That's all the questions we have for today. Don't forget to fix that basement window," she added on her way toward the front door. "Terrible idea, to leave it open that way."

With that, the detectives let themselves out. As soon as the door clicked shut, Frank sunk into the armchair, his body relaxing for the first time in the last hour.

"We need to get a lawyer," he said to Lisa and Malcolm.

Lisa was already on her way to the stove, plopping a pot of tea on to offer them all some comfort. "Honey," she shook her head. "You *are* a lawyer."

Frank kicked his feet up, his stomach churning with concern. "We need a better one."

CHAPTER TWENTY-FIVE

AFTER A QUIET DINNER at the diner— during which Annie had mostly entertained her own thoughts about the case— Annie and Ethan were back at their quaint motel, each of them on the landing outside their respective rooms. Ethan held a key in his hand, fiddling with it like he couldn't find the right end.

"You're buying time because you want to say something," Annie mentioned, glancing at the key.

"You know who did it," Ethan said. "But you haven't told me."

"I'll remind you, sir, that you're an agent of the law," Annie answered. "It would be unethical for me to tell you unless I was certain. Everything I suspect is still just suspicion. I need more facts."

"I can live with that," Ethan answered, leaning his back against the door to his motel room. "Wanna have dinner again?"

"We already ate," Annie stated.

"But you mostly thought the entire time. So that doesn't count." Ethan paused, considering. "What about ice cream?

You need dessert. All that thinking burns extra calories. You must be famished."

"And you?"

"I hardly think at all. It's why I have to work out."

"You afraid to go into your room alone?" Annie asked.

"Me? Of course not. Big strong guy," Ethan flexed a bicep. "But seeing Malcolm today, what he's been through. It's like us, isn't it? We're the same as him. Just haunted by things in the past. I sometimes think about it all and I just—"

He stopped speaking, mainly because Annie had strode towards him and put her hand over his mouth.

"Shh," she said. "I'll agree to ice cream. But only if we don't talk about the thing I can't talk about. Understand?"

He nodded, and she removed her hand from his mouth.

"You're buying," Ethan smiled at her. But there was a sadness behind his eyes. A sadness Annie knew neither one of them could shake. Ethan was haunted by the past in his waking hours, but for Annie, the nightmares about the past tended to arrive while she was asleep, uninvited and intrusive.

She would get the ice cream with Ethan, but only for him — not for herself, or her own state of mind. Because, unlike Ethan, Annie knew that she couldn't outrun the past. She knew she couldn't distract herself from what lay buried, deep in her subconscious. At least, not for long.

All she could do was try to solve each case that was presented to her, in the hopes it would lead her closer to fixing what was broken inside her. And if she couldn't fix it, she'd learn to live with it, just like Mr. Markin learned to live with his shame. She would help other people who had experienced what she had, because Annie knew what it was like to lose someone you loved to a violent crime.

And she would do everything in her power to make sure those who took an innocent life were brought to justice.

CHAPTER TWENTY-SIX

REGGIE

REGGIE SLAMMED the front door shut behind him as he stormed out of the home he shared with Janis. He strode across the lawn, letting his feet guide him toward a destination that remained unclear.

It couldn't be true. Janis— his wife, the woman he had built his home with— had just told him the unthinkable. Not only was she engaging in an affair, but she was having an affair of a certain kind. An affair with a woman. And worse yet, a neighbor.

He stumbled into the sea of black asphalt that constituted the cul-de-sac, trying to hold back a tsunami of rage. He wasn't angered so much by the fact Janis loved someone else. That, he could live with. It was that she had dared to do something so outside his moral compass. In selecting *her* as his wife, Reggie had taken a leap of faith. He had put his reputation in her hands. Janis was— in Reggie's opinion— an extension of himself and his legacy. And now, she had ruined it all.

How dare she, Reggie seethed, pulling his jacket tighter around his shoulders. His breath came out in spiraling billows as it melded with the crisp, evening air. Reggie tried to keep the pace of his gate even, in the hopes that— if any of the neighbors saw him— it would look like he was merely taking a walk.

He made the loop around Aspen Lane, passing the trees of its namesake bordering the edge of the iron gates. Normally, those gates assured Reggie of security. They were a symbol of the life he had worked so hard for. A life that promised him a certain level of stability, making him untouchable. But tonight, the gates reminded Reggie of the door to a cage. Tonight, the gates weren't keeping others out. They were locking Reggie *in.*

He curved past the outlet, acknowledging Otto's security booth, where a warm light radiated from a set of glass windows. His legs took him away from the entrance, forcing him North toward the top of the cul-de-sac, when suddenly, he saw it. Melissa and Sheila's upgraded home at the end of the street, with its obnoxious garage conversion laid bare for all to see. There were no curtains on the wide, sliding windows that had been added to the place where the garage door used to be, allowing the pottery wheel and enormous couch to be seen from the entrance to the community. The conversion had been undertaken with no consideration whatsoever to the neighborhood. The sound of construction. The banging day and night. Reggie had endured it all in the name of being neighborly, all so that the witch could have her pottery studio.

And the entire time, she was banging my wife. Reggie never thought he'd have to say those words. Hearing them in his own head was alarming, like he'd accidentally stepped into someone else's life.

Overcome, Reggie let his feet lead him toward the house. He was going to give those women a piece of his mind. He had been polite, up until now, but it was time to let them know what he really thought. He stomped across the lawn, overhead lights shining down at him as he invited himself to the home's front door. He clutched his hand into a fist, banging hard on the hand-carved wood. His chest heaved with the thrill of an impending confrontation, and he couldn't wait to get this evil out of him. He would feel relieved after it was done. The anger within him had turned to poison, and the only way to rid himself of it was to unleash the beast on someone else.

With a slow creak, the door opened. Reggie inhaled.

"You complete fucking bi--" he started to say, but he stopped, alarmed at what he saw in front of him.

There stood Melissa, tears pouring down her cheeks from underneath her glasses. Her brown, curly hair was tied back in a scrunchie, and she wore a robe loose and open over her pajamas. Her cheeks were flushed and she struggled to stand, presumably because of the Whiskey bottle she held in her left hand.

There was a long pause in which both Melissa and Reggie were too surprised to say anything. Then, Melissa broke the silence. "She told you, huh?"

The crack in Melissa's voice seemed to melt Reggie's rage. Her sadness mirrored something within him that he'd been suppressing. A deep, tragic pain of his own that he preferred to hide beneath anger, which was infinitely more productive. At the sight of her, that pain welled up, and Reggie felt a strange wetness on his face he hadn't experienced since he was a child.

"Everything's going to be different now," he heard himself say.

Melissa nodded. She held out the Whiskey bottle, and Reggie took it. He downed a swig, then followed Melissa into her home, directly into the office of his enemy. She ushered him into the living room and motioned to the couch.

"You can sit," she said vaguely, her eyes empty.

"Is Sheila here?" Reggie asked, afraid of what he might do if she was.

"She staying at her friend's house," Melissa answered. "Wanted to give me 'some space'," she made quotations in the air around the words *"some space,"* scoffing at the idea. "But the truth is, she just didn't even want to be around me anymore." Melissa stared at the ceiling as if there was a puzzle she could solve written on its surface. "Where did we go so wrong? I thought she loved me. She told me all these things I'd been doing that annoyed her. Apparently I talk about myself too much. Which is way off base because I'm a really good listener."

Reggie was about to say something but Melissa didn't notice and kept right on talking, the irony of which was not lost on Reggie.

"She said I'm an elitist and obsessed with my job, but like, hello?! I work in Academia. We're all intellectuals. What did she expect? She said I don't make her feel special and that I don't really *see her*. That she's just some appendage in my life. Which is so unfair!"

"Tell me about it," Reggie nodded. "Apparently I treat my wife like another appliance. I was accused of *ignoring her needs,* whatever the hell that means."

"Yeah, like, if you have so many needs speak up!" Melissa added, her words slurring a little. "I'm not a mind reader." She paused, straightening her robe as if it were an important fashion accessory. "The truth is, I'm not sensitive. Been a problem my whole life. Here I am, walking around as a woman, and I'm not *sensitive* enough. People hate it. That my outsides don't match my insides. But what am I supposed to do? I call things like they are. I live for *me.* I'm basically—" she motioned at Reggie, "*You.* But inside all of *this—"* she scanned her body with her hands. "It's a mismatch. Always has been. Always will be." She stretched, putting her feet up on the table. "I work hard. I provide for us while she makes her art or whatever. Hell, I let her build a pottery studio."

"That was nice," Reggie agreed.

"Not that nice," Melissa added. "I mostly did it to piss *you* off. Liked the idea you'd have to put up with construction. I loved it when you were so mad you even got Frank on board to protest—"

"I did," Reggie laughed. "Had him draw up legal papers to stop the build and everything. Slowed you down at least, didn't I?"

"You did."

"That was well-played," Reggie agreed, taking another swig of Whiskey. "You know how there's always a car parked in front of your house on trash day so you have to take your cans to the other side?"

"It's a long walk, yeah," Melissa acknowledged.

"That's me," Reggie said. "We keep my Dad's old beater in the garage. It's non-operational. And every week on trash day I get up at 6 a.m. to park it in front of your house. Just because I like that it means you have to drag those loaded cans further down the road. I wanted you to feel weak or something. Isn't that fucked?"

Melissa looked stunned for a second, then erupted into laughter. Before either of them knew what had happened, Reggie was laughing, too.

"You and me," Melissa said, breathless. "We both can't communicate. We both ignore our wives. And we both got cheated on." She grabbed the bottle of whiskey and poured herself another glass, letting the amber liquid soak the tumbler that sat on her table. "Never thought I'd see the day. You and me? We're more alike than we are different."

Reggie took this in, suddenly seeing Melissa in a new light. He had been quick to judge, because of her "lifestyle." But maybe it was true that the people we hate are the most like us. Sitting here in front of him was a comrade in arms.

This woman had provided for her wife. She had given her a good home, every day heading out into the world to battle the demands of capitalism. She was smart. Unafraid. And, fuck it— Reggie liked her.

"You and me," he held out a hand and Melissa shook it, the two of them suddenly united by what they'd just learned.

CHAPTER TWENTY-SEVEN

IT WAS three in the morning when Annie awoke with a start, pulling the blankets off her limp form to escape the rush of heat that surrounded her body. For a moment, the unfamiliar surroundings made Annie feel that she was still inside a dream. The motel coffee maker in the corner struck a strange figure. The alarm clock by her bed looked all wrong. The peeling ceiling paint seemed about to flake away in sheets. All of it was foreign, a strange, melting simulation of her bedroom back home.

Annie took a deep breath inwards, holding it for four seconds, just like the therapists had taught her as a teenager. She waited, allowing the breath to sit, then released it slowly.

"You are in a motel," she whispered aloud. "You are touching the blankets. You are lying on the bed." These things helped to ground her. Naming her surroundings brought her back to the moment when she'd had a dream like this one. The problem, of course, was that Annie's nightmares weren't dreams at all. They were memories, embedded deep in her subconscious with painstaking attention to specific details.

That was the beauty and the curse of Annie's mind, which had always shown an innate propensity for cataloging tiny elements in a broad picture. Growing up, she'd counted the cans in their family pantry with merely a glance, forever remembering that on Tuesday the 25th of March, there were twenty cans, but by Wednesday the 36th, only eighteen. When her mother purchased a new woven quilt for her bedroom, Annie became so obsessed with the tangled pattern of the threads in the fabric that it had to be taken away for fear that Annie might never sleep again. Her obsession with disparate parts extended to people as well. Annie remembered everything about everyone. Birthdays. Likes and dislikes. Favorite colors. She could take the individual elements that made up a person and stack them on top of one another instead of interacting with the cohesive whole. It was all without trying. Annie had never *wanted* to experience the world this way, but it was how she'd been wired, and now— as an adult— she'd learned to use it to her advantage.

She rolled to the side of the bed and put her feet on the ground, letting her heels sink into the dirty motel carpet. Annie knew what she was going to do before she did it, and judged herself for it right away. Still, against her protests, Annie's legs firmed and her body rose, floating toward the door to her motel room. She opened it, the cold night air a shock to her body, which was protected only by a thin nightgown.

She stepped outside, letting the door click shut behind her. Her skin prickled as she moved toward the front door to the room behind her, where she knew Ethan lay sleeping, probably snoring in that quiet way of his. Ethan slept like he was apologizing for being tired, with stifled, half-hearted snorts and a body that flipped around so much it still seemed partly awake.

Annie stood at his door, not bothering to knock. She touched the handle. Turned the knob. The door floated open. Ethan had left it unlocked, probably because he had seen the look in her eye earlier that evening when they'd gone to their respective rooms. He had known she would need him, even before she'd known it herself.

Annie pushed open the door, revealing Ethan, sitting up in his bed.

"Again?" he asked.

Annie nodded. Ethan pulled back the comforter, inviting her in. Without a word, Annie moved toward him, crawling underneath the blankets. Ethan put his arm around her, creating a space for her to press into him and forget herself.

For a while, they didn't talk. Ethan just held Annie close, gently running his thumb over the back of her hand, which he held in his with gentle care.

"I hoped this would be our chance to solve it," Annie whispered. "This one felt different."

"I know," Ethan agreed. "Annie, it's possible— the case has been closed for so many years. We may never solve it—"

"Don't say that," Annie cut him off. "You can't *ever* say that." "I still dream about it too," Ethan answered.

The admission hit Annie like a punch to the stomach. She'd been open about her nightmares because she'd needed Ethan's support in moments like this. But he had never told her still had them, too.

The nightmare that was really a memory came flooding back to Annie in flashes. The house. Her brother, his body on the floor of the immaculate home, staged to be sold. Ethan's sister, her image splayed across missing posters. The cameras. The newspapers. The search, finding nothing.

Annie was only sixteen when the crime happened. She'd heard about the killer on the news before it ever affected her personally— they'd called him the "Real Estate Ripper"— a serial murderer who seemed to target people in their homes, especially when that home was listed for sale. Somehow, either the buyer or the seller would turn up dead, with nothing but a white envelope and a three-word letter within, meant to confuse authorities and send them in the wrong direction.

Ethan's older sister was so proud of the small condo she'd purchased. It was a starter home. She was there, signing the papers to close the sale from the town's newest Real Estate agent— Annie's brother.

Annie's brother was new to adulthood when it happened, and still lived at home. She remembered him sitting at the breakfast table that day, telling Annie and her parents that closing this deal meant his business was taking off. He felt like the future was his.

Until it wasn't.

She remembered the images splashed across television screens of his body, stomach down, head bleeding. Her parents had tried to shield her from it, but of course, Annie hadn't been able to hide from the nationwide coverage. And Ethan's sister was never found, her face plastered on "missing" posters for years to come. She was gone, with nothing but a white envelope and a brief, handwritten letter within. It read, simply "Because they knew."

The police didn't know what to make of it, and the case was never solved.

Ethan and Annie had been connected by an invisible string that day. Both of them found themselves at the center of a media frenzy. Each of them was caught publicly mourning the loss of a sibling. They'd been acquaintances up until the crime, but afterward— they'd become friends. Ethan had protected Annie from the kids at school who dared to comment on what had happened. And Annie had helped Ethan as he failed his classes, doing not just her own assignments, but also his. They had the kind of loyalty between them that came only with surviving trauma. They were like soldiers who had been to war together.

The crime had changed both their lives forever. It was what made Ethan join the FBI, and what called Annie to open up her private investigator shingle. But even as life pulled them down their respective paths, the two old friends had never forgotten the promise they'd made each other:

One day, they would solve the case that brought them together.

"Try Aspen Lane," Annie whispered aloud. "It was even three letters. It *has* to be connected. It just doesn't make sense otherwise." Annie hated it when the pieces were all there, but the picture they built didn't live up to what she'd envisioned. She was missing something. There was no other explanation. "If I could just look at it the right way I could figure it out. There's something I haven't seen yet. Some piece that will make it all fall into place."

Ethan kissed the top of her head, pulling her closer.

"Sometimes things just don't make sense. Let it be," he said, noting how she stiffened at the suggestion. Then, he added, "Just for tonight. Not forever."

At that, Annie relaxed, letting herself give up the battle to win the war. She closed her eyes, leaning into the one person — the only person— who had ever been able to make sense of the most unsolvable puzzle. The one Annie struggled with each day. The one within herself.

CHAPTER TWENTY-EIGHT

LIGHT FILTERED in from behind the motel's dusty curtains, signaling a new day. Annie rolled over in bed, noticing her discomfort at being in Ethan's room. The secrets she kept close only felt safe when shared underneath the blanket of night. When revealed in the context of a new day, they were too vulnerable to be exposed. Annie's weaknesses embarrassed her. She felt a pang of regret, like the kind that came from a night out drinking or a one-night stand. All she had done was share a moment of vulnerability with a man who had known her most of her life— but the maneuver felt like a sin against the woman she'd promised herself she would become. The woman who didn't need anyone.

She hoped Ethan would act as if nothing had happened.

Thankfully for Annie, Ethan wasn't there. She looked over her shoulder, finding nothing but the other half of the bed, perfectly made. The purring of the in-wall heating unit was the only sound in the room besides Annie's own breathing.

Annie stood, taking the comforter with her like a shawl wrapped around her shoulders. She made her way to the coffee table, her perfect memory recreating the scene from the night before. Last night, Ethan's wallet and keys had been on the edge of the table, next to the lamp. Now, both were missing.

He'd left her alone in the room. Just the way he knew she would have wanted it.

Relieved at the lack of company, Annie dropped the comforter and stepped into the bathroom. She turned on the shower, entering the little cave and letting the hot water run over her skin.

She thought about the facts of her case. She was almost done with her investigation into Mr. Markin's murder. At this point, Annie had solved all three points of the investigation, though she needed the appropriate evidence to make her conclusions undeniable. Annie believed she knew who killed Mr. Markin, although she lacked the necessary forensic evidence to support her claim. She knew who committed the robbery, and had defined its connection to Mr. Markin's ultimate demise. And she knew who sent the letter hiring her to join the case, although the answer had not been what she'd hoped for.

Annie was almost ready to share her findings, except for one small puzzle piece she just couldn't make fit.

The murder weapon.

The forensics report had revealed Mr. Markin was shot by a specific type of handgun. A Colt Model 1911A1, to be exact. The gun was a standard issue item during the 1970s, used by the United States Military during the Vietnam War. It was an interesting choice, given the proliferation of weapons with greater firing power and more modern advantages.

Annie knew that— to make her case ironclad and ensure the person responsible for Mr. Markin's death was held accountable— she needed to trace the origins of the murder weapon and connect it with the killer. Until then, she couldn't share her findings with anyone. Not even with Ethan. Before she offered her conclusions, she needed to be sure.

Annie stepped out of the shower, firm in her resolve. She

dried her hair— still considering the facts of the case— then stepped into her clothes from the day before. She paused at Ethan's suitcase before reaching inside and pulling out one of his flannel shirts. She popped it over her tank top, creating what amounted to a brand-new outfit. Then, she stepped out of the motel, locking the doorknob from the inside before letting it shut behind her.

She marched down the stairs toward the parking lot. There, Ethan leaned on the hood of his black, unmarked FBI-issued vehicle, holding a coffee in each hand. Ethan looked as if the events of the night before were forgotten. Annie wondered if he'd learned to embrace her cycle of moving closer toward him, then farther away. Last night wasn't the first time she had met him at his hotel door, but this morning was the first time he'd seemed to let it go without attachment.

"Thought you'd want a moment alone before I shared the news," he smiled at her. Annie took the coffee, grateful.

"News?"

"They're reading the will today."

"Who's invited?" Annie asked.

"Seems Mr. Markin left a little something to the entire neighborhood."

"Guess we'd better join them," Annie laughed, opening the door to the vehicle's passenger side.

"Of course," Ethan answered, pushing the start button so the engine roared to life. "I'd hate to miss a show."

CHAPTER TWENTY-NINE

THE NEIGHBORS LOOKED ALARMED to find themselves back in the country club's conference room. Annie could understand why. In many ways, this place— with its tiered fountains and carved statues surrounded by perfectly green grass— represented a certain kind of immunity. There was a sense of safety in the confines of the country club, as if earning membership could spare someone from experiencing the roughest edge of the knife of life. Now, that safety had been interrupted— brought into question in a way that violated the neighborhood's most sacred spaces.

Attendance at the reading of the will— as prescribed by the executor of Mr. Markin's estate— was optional. Every resident of Aspen Lane had been contacted via phone by Laemle & Leamle, Esq., the law firm handling Mr. Markin's affairs. They'd been notified that they were named as recipients but given no other information. Instead, they were merely informed it was Mr. Markin's wish that they all be present to hear the reading.

Now, they were sitting in a circle in one of the country club's mirrored conference rooms, their chairs arranged in front of a long table. Behind the table sat Mr. Laemle, an old friend of Mr. Markin's who also happened to be his lawyer. Mr. Laemle wore a suit and tie for the affair, and conducted himself with nothing but the utmost professionalism. He was a small, mustached man, and he exhibited a somewhat judicial aura, as if he carried the sanctity of the law with him wherever he went. He clicked open a crocodile-skin briefcase, clearing his throat as he extracted a set of papers within.

"You'll understand the reading of this will is in accordance with Mr. Markin's wishes," Mr. Laemle stated. "He had his estate well-managed and was exceptionally clear when it came to the ultimate handling of his affairs."

A few nods rippled throughout the room. In front of him, the neighbors presented a rather motley crew. Krystal played with the edge of a handkerchief tied to her hair, unable to stop fidgeting.

"Will this take like, very long?" Krystal asked, voice trembling a little. "I have a reading to get to, and the future doesn't wait."

"No time at all," Mr. Laemle reassured her. "We'll get straight to business."

"Great," Krystal answered. Beside her, Jared allowed his leg to bounce up and down, while his brothers fussed with the settings on a video camera.

"No recording will be permitted," Mr. Laemle said to Jared's brothers. Edmonte set the camera down, a defiant look in his eyes.

"Who are you to tell us what we can and can't film—" Edmonte started to say, but he was interrupted by an elbow from Jared, sent straight to his ribs.

"Knock it off," Jared muttered. "Just let him get this over with."

"Get it over with is right," Reggie responded. He was sitting at the end of the collection of chairs, Melissa seated beside him instead of his wife. The two of them had their arms crossed, looking like mirror images of each other, both of them dressed in button-down shirts and glasses. The resemblance wasn't lost on Janis and Sheila, who were seated on the opposite end of the room, occasionally stealing glances at their ex-partners.

"Downright alarming isn't it?" Sheila whispered into Janis's ear, acknowledging the way Reggie and Melissa seemed to mirror one another. Janis shushed her, but inwardly couldn't deny she'd been thinking the same thing.

In the center of the group sat Frank, Lisa, and Malcolm, who had decided to attend the meeting with his parents. Frank raised a hand in greeting at two familiar figures leaning against the back wall: Annie and Ethan. They oversaw the meeting as if they were patrons at the zoo, looking at animals in glass cages. Annie waved back at Frank, her ever-pleasant expression unchanged. Frank told himself it was productive to be on excellent terms with the detectives, but he was worried about his son's ever-growing connection to the crime. So worried, in fact, that last night he'd reached out to an old friend in criminal law, and retained a lawyer for his son. But he was hoping it wouldn't come to that. He wasn't reassured, however, given the presence of two additional figures positioned to the left and right of Mr. Laemle:

Police Officers.

One, Frank recognized as Chief Hardgrave. He had met her many years ago when he was Aspen Lane's representative at the local neighborhood watch, and she had come to speak to the club about creating secure communities. He'd found her to be competent and efficient, if not overly concerned with the next election cycle. Beside her stood a young man in uniform— young enough that he looked to be early in his tenure as an officer. The lack of decoration on his blues told Frank this man was there as Hardgrave's backup, though her muscular frame indicated she'd hardly need it. The presence of law enforcement struck Frank as overkill at a simple reading of a will, but perhaps they expected some kind of outrage or brawl to break out.

"Now," Mr. Laemle began, his words snapping Frank back into the present moment. "Let's get to it." He cleared his throat, and all the air seemed to leave the room. A strange quiet settled over the group. "Each of you is present today because you are, in some form or another, named in Mr. Markin's last Will and Testament. The will was notarized and signed in person at my office in the presence of a witness, and a copy was filed with the superior court. Its allocations are final."

Mr. Laemle adjusted his glasses, glanced down at the will, and began to read. "To my community, mentioned in this will. I'd like to say how much you all have meant to me. I learned as a young man what it meant to be a part of a team, and I never forgot the value of putting the group before oneself. Thank you, for what you contributed to my life, and for allowing me to add to yours."

Frank could almost imagine the words in Mr. Markin's characteristic low rumble. It was strange, how the cadence of someone's voice could carry over to the written word. He glanced around the room to see if anyone else felt the same, and was surprised at the emotion he found there. Krystal had her hand over her mouth, tears streaming down her cheeks. It looked like she was struggling to catch her breath, each sharp inhale delivering just enough air to lead to the next moment. Next to her, Jared's face was flushed, his eyes turned toward the ceiling like he might lose it at any moment. At the far end of the hall, Janis and Sheila leaned on one another, a slight tremble running through Janis's fingers, which clutched the end of Sheila's sweater. Even Reggie appeared affected by the seriousness of the moment, his arms now uncrossed and laying limp on his lap as if he had resigned himself to fate, having finally accepted that nothing in life was able to be changed by his own efforts.

"To the Key Club of Watersborough," Mr. Laemle continued, "I leave ten thousand dollars, to be used for any and all charitable activities as they see fit. To the Friendship Society of the Thirty-Second Legion, I leave ten thousand dollars, also to be used for any and all charitable activities as they see fit. To my brothers, there, I'd like to add that I apologize for taking so long to find my way home. Thank you for greeting me with open arms when I finally knocked at your door." Mr. Laemle paused, as if he knew he was arriving at the moment the entire room had been waiting for.

"To the residents of Aspen Lane, I leave thirty thousand dollars, to be used for improvement of the street, botany, and general upkeep of the gates and community spaces." Gasps and small mutters filled the room. At the back wall, Annie watched each individual reaction from every resident of the neighborhood. Based on the surprised expressions, no one had expected this. "I request that additional Aspen trees be planted around the entrance to our street," Mr. Laemmle continued, "Creating a space for birds and increasing the sense of privacy in this small enclave. As a resident of Aspen Lane for more than thirty years, I've never felt more at home than I did with all of you. The executor of my will is charged with managing the funds and will approve access requests for community improvement projects on a case-by-case basis. As to my house itself..." Mr. Laemle hesitated, blowing his nose into a handkerchief, which he then stuffed into his pocket. "I leave the property, the furniture, and all equitable interest within... to Mr. Malcolm Havvendish."

Heads whipped around as all eyes in the room landed on — Malcolm. Frank could feel his heart pounding in his ears. Normally, it would be a blessing for someone to inherit a house from a friend. But, given the circumstances of the murder and the missing weapon, Frank didn't feel this was a lucky moment for his son.

"Me?" Malcolm asked, shock rippling through the edges

of his voice. No one answered him, and Malcolm was left to sit in his surprise, his mouth still hanging open as the gravity of what had just happened became apparent.

"I hope this gift allows him to start fresh, close to his family, in the neighborhood he thought he could never afford," Mr. Laemle concluded.

From there, time seemed to speed up. Mr. Laemle finished the will by reading the final sentence. "The remainder of my estate will be left to the Boys and Girls Club of Watersborough. I hope these contributions can be used to support future generations," he droned, but at this point, no one was listening. There were a few more words exchanged and a clicking sound as Mr. Laemle slid the will back into his briefcase and shut the lid as if declaring the show was over. The moment the reading was finished, Chief Hardgrave moved around the table like a leopard on the prowl. Frank stood, pulling his son up by the arm, Lisa on the other side, the two of them dragging Malcolm toward the double doors that marked their exit. But they weren't fast enough.

Hardgrave beat them to the exit, her badge in hand. She flashed it at them, and the trio stopped in their tracks.

"Malcolm Havvendish?" She asked.

"That's me," Malcolm answered, not a shred of fear in his voice. Instead, his tone was resigned.

"Are you the registered owner of a Colt 1911 handgun?"

"I am," Malcolm confirmed.

"Can you allow us to examine that gun?"

"To be honest," Malcolm swallowed. "I don't know where it is right now."

Frank cringed, absolute dread rushing through his body. *We should have told them the moment we realized the gun was missing,* Frank thought, disgusted with himself for how stupid he'd been. He would have advised any client to go to the police immediately, but when it came to his son, he'd been blinded by love. By the desire to protect. And now, he'd set his child up for failure. Frank had never hated himself so much.

"This is a misunderstanding—" Frank started to say, but Office Hardgrave held up a hand, silencing him.

"He can speak for himself," she added, and at once Frank knew this woman had already decided his son was guilty. She turned back to Malcolm, motioning to her colleague for backup. Another Officer appeared from nowhere, pulling Malcolm's hands behind his back. "Malcolm Havvendish, you are under arrest for the murder of Mr. Harold Markin." Officer Hardgrave locked a pair of handcuffs onto Malcolm's wrists, leading him through the double doors as she went. "You have the right to remain silent. Anything you say can and will be used against you. You have the right to an attorney. If you cannot afford one, one will appointed for you..."

Frank listened to the Miranda rights, watching as his son gave one helpless look over his shoulder, disappearing through the doorway.

"Don't say anything, son!" Frank called after him, trying to make sure Malcolm heard him over the sounds of Lisa crying. "Not a word! It's going to be okay. Everything's going to be okay!'

The lie left his mouth with ease, even though he knew, without a doubt, that absolutely nothing was going to be okay. Frank turned, facing the room. There, his neighbors stood, eyes wide, completely shocked at what had just happened. For a moment, nobody did anything. Then, Reggie stepped forward.

"We'll get him out, Frank," he said, putting a hand on his shoulder. "Everybody here knows it wasn't Malcolm."

The room erupted in agreement all at the same time.

"I can read his cards," Krystal offered, rummaging through her purse to find a deck, which she immediately spread out over a chair.

"We'll put it on the internet," Jared said, his brother still holding the video camera, which had presumably captured everything. "Innocent man accused of crime. We'll go viral and collect money for a defense. We'll get him out—"

"I can see if the University has a connection to the Innocence Project," Melissa added.

The neighbors cawed like a flock of seagulls, each of them throwing one idea over the other until Detective Annie Hudson's voice cut through the crowd.

"It seems," Annie said, without much volume at all. "It's almost time for me to share my conclusions."

Everyone stared at her as if they'd forgotten she was there. She turned to Ethan, who stood behind her, always in her wake. "Is there anything you can do in the short term?" She asked.

"I can slow them down," Ethan offered. "I can claim Jurisdictional issues interfering with an ongoing investigation with the FBI. But I can't stop them forever. They have a right to bring charges if the D.A. thinks they have enough evidence."

Annie nodded, then stepped forward, speaking directly to Frank and Lisa.

"By her body language and, from what I know about the way she operates, Officer Hardgrave will have every reason to make her case against Malcolm as swiftly as possible," Annie stated, regret etched across her eyes. "To make sure he walks, I'll have to play a bit of a game." She paused, letting the moment sit. "Do I have your permission, to do what I need to do to flush out the real killer? It might mean your son stays in custody for a brief period. But when he goes free—he'll *truly* be free. He'll be exonerated, beyond a reasonable doubt."

Frank and Lisa exchanged a look, both of them aghast that they'd ended up in such a predicament.

"Do everything you can," Frank said to Annie. She nodded and, with that, the reading of the will was over.

CHAPTER THIRTY

"FORENSICS MATCHED the bullet hole to a very specific pistol," Chief Hardgrave said, leaning against a window situated in the interior of Watersborough's police station. On the other side of the glass, Malcolm was seated at a metal table, his hands uncuffed, a paper cup of coffee in front of him. He was alone in the room, his face expressionless. He'd been in battle before, and it showed. He never glanced once at the double-sided mirror in front of him, although he certainly knew he was being watched from the other side. His resolve was cool and steely. To Chief Hardgrave, it looked a hell of a lot like guilt.

"The bullet extracted in the autopsy belonged to a Colt 1911," Hardgrave added. "We ran a search through the gun registry for any owners in the area, and imagine our surprise when Malcolm popped up. Not only does he own the gun, he lives in very same community as Mr. Markin. Doesn't that strike you as odd?" She shook her head at Annie and Ethan, who were standing across from her, looking out of place in the station's observation room.

"Suspicions aren't facts," Annie replied, congenial as ever.

"You've settled on Malcolm— that much is clear. But the evidence points overwhelmingly in another direction."

"The evidence," Officer Hardgrave scoffed, "points at Malcolm. As we speak, a group of officers is searching his home. The gun will be there, his fingerprints all over it."

"The gun *won't* be there," Annie told her. "I could see it on their faces after I interviewed the family. They gave off the physical indicators of deception. Eyes looking away from me. Fidgeting. They said the gun was out for cleaning, but their body language said it's missing."

"Because he disposed of it after committing the crime."

"Because somebody *else* took the gun, hoping to pin it all on Malcolm," Annie corrected her.

"And the family didn't think to report it?"

"Malcolm's been through a lot," Annie answered. "He's a grown man who's survived combat everyone in this room can only imagine. But his father, like so many parents, still sees him as a child. A child he's trying to protect. They didn't come forward because my presence complicated things. Surely they felt the addition of a Detective into the mix complicated the situation."

"They're not the only ones," Hardgrave answered, rolling her eyes.

Annie pressed on. "He's innocent. We just need to flush out the killer."

"And how do you suggest we do that?"

Annie glanced at Ethan, who cleared his throat, preparing for the hard sell. "The FBI would like to issue a public announcement, in coordination with the Watersborough Police Department. This was classified earlier, but I've gotten the go-ahead to share with you now..." He reached into Annie's bag, pulling out a file, which he handed to Chief Hardgrave. "We believe this case may be related to a series of murders committed fifteen years ago."

"The Real Estate Ripper?" Hardgrave asked as she flipped through the file, examining the case information within.

"Yes," Ethan confirmed. "He left a three-word letter at the scene of each crime. Black ink on white paper. Each one the same."

"The case was never solved," Hardgrave read aloud, frustration in her tone. Caring for her immediate community was enough. Asking her to care about a serial killer who was last active a decade ago was too much. "What does this have to do with our murder?"

"Annie was hired to investigate Aspen Lane by a similar letter."

"I thought the FBI hired her," Hardgrave asked, suddenly concerned.

"We did," Ethan assured her. "But Annie received the letter— along with some cash— in advance of the murder becoming public knowledge. She brought it to us, and we assigned her to help with the case." He clocked Hardgrave's face, her expression horrified. "Her track record is impeccable. We've worked with her before. The letter was extraneous."

Hardgrave laughed. "More than that, it bears no relevance. The letter could be a copycat—"

"The FBI believes it's the original, given Annie's history," he glanced at Annie as if asking for permission. She gave a slight nod.

"Her history?"

"Annie is connected to one of the murders committed by the Real Estate Ripper," he paused. "Her brother was a victim."

Hardgrave took this in, allowing a long sigh to escape her lips. She turned away from them, her hands reaching for her temples. It had been a long week. She'd been looking forward to making the announcement they'd arrested a potential suspect. She'd already imagined the press conference, cameras from the local News Station poised at the ready. How easy it would be to reassure the community, now that the killer had been brought into custody. If she allowed Annie and Ethan to have their way, the vision crumbled.

"What do you need from me?" she asked.

"We'd like you to issue a statement that you won't be filing charges until you find the murder weapon," Ethan answered. "It needs to be public, issued across every TV station in the county. As for reach and press, the FBI can help with that."

Hardgrave considered his offer. There was no reason she couldn't combine her public announcement with what he asked. The FBI's ability to reach national news might carry her message even further than she'd anticipated. *Local Chief of Police makes arrest in dangerous case.* The potential headline played through her imagination with a musical tenor.

"That might be possible," Hardgrave agreed. "What else?"

"Release Malcolm," Ethan added. Hardgrave started to object, but Ethan pushed forward. "You don't have enough to hold him. He's innocent, a war veteran—"

"How about this?" Hardgrave interjected. "I'll hold my press conference and announce that we're holding the subject for questioning. Assuming my officers haven't found the gun after a thorough search of his home—"

"They *won't*," Annie added.

"—I'll state that we feel we have enough evidence to proceed but are seeking information about the whereabouts of the murder weapon. I'll offer a reward for anyone who has information about the gun. Sound fair?"

"We need to make the killer feel like Malcolm won't be prosecuted unless the gun turns up," Ethan replied.

"It's the best I can offer," Hardgrave said, crossing her arms and leaning against the wall, her voice sounding like a car salesman's. "Take it or leave it."

Ethan and Annie exchanged a glance, considering the deal.

"We'll take it," Annie said. She shook Hardgrave's hand, sealing Malcolm's fate in a single moment.

CHAPTER THIRTY-ONE

KRYSTAL

KRYSTAL WAS MAKING a chia seed parfait when the story came on the news. She was halfway through adding a mixture of fruits and spices— all known for their healing properties— when Malcolm's face appeared on her living room television, which had been set to the nightly news. An image of Aspen Lane appeared, those familiar iron gates that usually felt comforting suddenly made threatening when broadcast on the local news. Krystal grabbed the remote control, turning up the volume so she could hear the report.

"... a special press conference, held by Police Chief Hardgrave," a pithy female news anchor said before the screen cutaway to what appeared to be live footage of Chief Hardgrave, standing in front of a collection of flashing cameras on the steps outside of the Watersborough Police Department.

Krystal ran to the couch, sitting in her usual spot and curling her legs up underneath her, using a fringed pillow to bolster their position. She struck a match from a box on the end table, lighting a nearby stick of incense and inserting it into its holder. Given this new development, she was committed to creating good energy.

"We've taken the subject custody, and are currently

holding him for questioning," Chief Hardgrave said from the TV screen. Krystal couldn't help but notice that she looked pleased to be delivering the news that Malcolm had been taken into her hands. "It is the department's position that the motive is clear, given that he was named a main recipient in the subject's will."

We were all in the will, Krystal thought. *Why don't you come for the whole neighborhood then?* She chided herself for the momentary lapse in judgment. How stupid, to invite in the negative. She was already at risk, given the agreement she'd had with Mr. Markin. Yes, she'd destroyed the evidence of their arrangement, but there was still a possibility— however small— that she might be exposed. This possibility was even greater now that the case was receiving national attention.

On the television screen, Chief Hardgrave paused. Then, teeth-gritted, she stated, "We are currently seeking the murder weapon, which forensics has identified as a Colt 1911 handgun. After a search of the subject's home, the gun was not found."

They couldn't find the gun? Krystal considered, wondering if this was good news for Malcolm.

"We consider locating the murder weapon a high priority next step in bringing charges against Mr. Malcolm Havvendish," Hardgrave continued. "We urge any citizens with information about the firearm to reach out to us. This matter is of such pivotal importance to our investigation that, in cooperation with the FBI, we're offering a $20,000 reward for anyone who supplies information that leads to the location of the weapon."

Krystal wafted the incense closer, inhaling its sweet aroma. She didn't think Malcolm was guilty. She was sure he wasn't. But despite that, some small part of her wished she knew anything useful— anything at all— about that gun.

Because, right now, she could really use that twenty-thousand dollars.

CHAPTER THIRTY-TWO

REGGIE

REGGIE WAS BANGING on an old jukebox in his least favorite bar when the news story about Malcolm appeared above his head, broadcast on the flat-screen that hung above the mirrored wall at O'Reilly's pub. O'Reilly's was the place Reggie stopped between leaving work and heading home. It was a sanctuary of sorts, a pit-stop for Reggie when he needed a breather between his work responsibilities and his home life. He'd gotten into trouble, here— there was no denying that. Occasionally, he'd met a woman on a chair beside him and allowed himself to chat with her just a little too long. Maybe even traded numbers. It never led to anything, but it made Reggie feel like he still had appeal. That was the irony of Janis' transgression. Reggie had of course had his opportunities in the past. He'd just turned them down out of duty— an idea apparently completely foreign to Janis.

Reggie looked up at the screen, watching as Malcolm's face appeared in an insert box beside the newscaster. He couldn't make out what she was saying, but he knew it had to do with Aspen Lane. He wondered how all of this would affect his property values, especially now that he and Janis were separating and might have to sell the house. He wouldn't let *her* keep their home, if he had his way.

"Hey," Reggie said to the bartender, flagging him down. "Turn it up?"

The bartender stopped wiping out a glass long enough to retrieve the remote from a drawer. He pointed it at the screen, and the story echoed across the bar.

"... and now, we'll head to our correspondent, live at the scene," the news anchor on the television said. The screen cutaway to a wide shot of Watersborough Police Department. Reggie recognized Chief Hardgrave from the reading of the will, standing at a podium positioned at the top of the steps. As she began her prepared remarks, Reggie gave up on the jukebox, retreating to his seat now that something more relevant to his own life had emerged.

He reached the bar, plopping down on a stool next to his date for the evening: Melissa. She kicked back her second beer, holding up a finger to the bartender.

"Another," she said.

"How many hours are we at?" Reggie asked.

"Around three," Melissa answered.

"Think they miss us yet?" Reggie had taken to referencing his soon-to-be-ex-wife only by pronouns such as "she," "her," or even, "the witch." When he was forced to refer to Janis and Sheila as a pair, he relied only on "they" or "them," as if the betrayals committed by the pair had wiped away his memory of their actual names.

"Probably not," Melissa said. "But I still don't want to go home."

"You see the story on Malcolm?" Reggie pointed at the television.

Melissa leaned forward, listening to Chief Hardgrave's request as it blasted across the bar. "They're looking for the murder weapon?" She smirked, chugging some of her fresh beer, compliments of the bartender. "That night was so weird," she said, remembering.

"What do you mean?" Reggie asked, his curiosity piqued.

"Nothing just," she was tipsy, swiveling on her seat. "Well, I guess I can tell you now. Because we're brothers, right?"

"Right," Reggie confirmed, skin prickling.

"And I don't have any reason to be loyal to— *her*," Melissa continued, referencing Sheila without using her name, just as Reggie had done. "After how she's treated me."

"Of course not," Reggie confirmed. "We owe them nothing."

"Thing was, I lied when I told the detectives we were intimate the night Mr. Markin was killed. That wasn't true at all," Melissa slurred. "The truth was, I was all alone, in the bathtub. And the loud music that was playing? That was just for me. I do it all the time when Sheila and I fight. She yells. I yell. Then I go into the bathroom and slam the door shut. I fill the tub up high and blast my music, so she knows I can't hear anything she says and she's not allowed to talk to me anymore."

"Okay," Reggie said, drawing the word out long to indicate he still didn't see the point.

"What's weird was, when I came out of the bathroom that night, something was wrong with Sheila. She'd been in her pottery studio, making some stupid bowl," Melissa waved a hand in the air. "But when I came out of the tub, she was sitting on the living room couch... *crying."*

"Crying?" Reggie repeated.

"Yeah. She looked like she'd see a ghost. I thought maybe it was over our fight, but she'd never cried about us before," Melissa scoffed, taking another gulp of her drink. "Would probably be too much to ask for her to give a fuck, wouldn't it?"

"What was she crying about?"

"She wouldn't say," Melissa answered. "She just curled up

on the couch, her cheeks all red, tears streaming down her cheeks. She kept saying, 'There's nothing I can do to change it now anyway.'"

Reggie inhaled, alarmed by this new information.

"And you didn't think to tell the police?" He asked, horrified at what Melissa had done.

"Why?" Melissa shrugged. "Sheila's an artist. She gets..." Melissa made the sign for 'crazy,' circling a finger in the air by her ear. "She probably broke her stupid bowl or something and decided to be emotionally crushed by it for a few days. I didn't think it was that weird until the Detectives started poking around. But even then, I didn't say anything because — come on. It's not like Sheila's a *murderer.*" Melissa laughed at the idea.

Reggie didn't say anything.

"She might be a cheater," Melissa said. "But she's not a *murderer."* There was a long pause. "Right?"

There was a moment in which Melissa and Reggie exchanged a loaded glance. The truth was, the two of them had been wrong about their spouses before. They'd shared homes with people they'd barely bothered to get to know, or *see,* on any deep level. If Sheila was capable of cheating and lying about it, who knew what other crimes she might have committed in secret?

"We're going to need another round," Reggie said, waving at the bartender once again.

CHAPTER THIRTY-THREE

JANIS & SHEILA

JANIS AND SHEILA were curled up together on the couch when the story about Malcolm appeared as a news alert on Sheila's phone. They'd been spending blissful, uninterrupted time together since they broke the news to their spouses, who had conveniently been coming home late ever since. As far as the children went, Janis had sat both boys down and told them Mommy needed to be herself, and that meant some life changes. They'd seemed unmoved by the information, but they were both so young Janis couldn't be sure they understood the situation in its entirety. She hoped to make their lives as uninterrupted as possible during the impending separation, perhaps by staying in the house on Aspen Lane— if Reggie wouldn't fight her on it, which Janis was sure he would. Reggie had continued to leave Janis with the full responsibility of caring for their children while he processed his feelings about what she had done. But Janis knew when it came to material assets, Reggie would suddenly find the energy to care. Janis didn't want the house because of its monetary value, but only because keeping it would mean continuing to raise the boys in a place they were used to being. She had held off on introducing the boys to Sheila until she was sure the relationship would be permanent. They were already asleep, upstairs, by the time she asked Sheila to come over, and if they happened to wake up and waddle toward the living room, Janis figured she could always tell them Sheila was a neighbor. After all, it wouldn't be a lie.

"They're looking for the gun," Sheila said out of nowhere, reading off the news alert on her phone. "They've offered a reward." Sheila paused, thinking about what happened the night Mr. Markin was killed. "Are you sure we shouldn't say anything publicly?"

Janis shook her head. "The detective— Annie— she said she has a plan to flush out the killer. She'll need us to be honest but at the proper time."

"And you trust her?"

Janis considered this. "I do," she said. "It seemed like she genuinely empathized with us. She'll do the right thing."

"And Malcolm?" Sheila asked. "He gets to sit in prison while we all wait?"

"You and I both know what that's like, don't we?" Janis said. "It's the only way to make sure. They have to prove it was someone else, beyond a reasonable doubt."

"Our testimony wouldn't be enough?" Sheila prodded.

Janis rolled her eyes. "Hello, grand jury," she stood, imitating a lawyer. "I'd like to introduce you to our best witnesses! Two lying lesbians who were in the middle of having an affair when they saw Mr. Markin get shot in cold blood." She adjusted a fake tie, pacing back and forth across the living room. "They were having sex with the curtains open when they saw their neighbor get murdered by someone they both know. They lied to their spouses about the affair, and *also* lied directly to Detectives when questioned—"

"True," Sheila laughed. "I see your point."

Janis collapsed on the couch, the humor of the moment giving way to a deeper darkness. "We discredited ourselves by not going to the police right away."

Janis remembered the night it had happened. They'd been in Sheila's pottery studio, where they met whenever possible. Sheila and Melissa had just fought and— as twisted as it was — their fights always made Sheila more likely to call. When Janis had arrived, they'd been so hungry for each other and in such a rush, they hadn't noticed the curtains that typically covered the large windows in the front of the studio were open. In all honesty, Janis *might* have noticed the curtains weren't pulled shut, but didn't bother to say anything because Aspen Lane was such a quiet street— no one was ever out that late. Or maybe, as she'd thought many times since the murder, she hadn't bothered to close the curtains because a part of her felt so guilty about what she was doing that she secretly wanted to get caught and end the suffering for all involved.

Either way, it was in the middle of an embrace that Janis and Sheila heard the gunshot. It was a single shot, rippling throughout the cul-de-sac like the crackling of a firework. Janis remembered the way they'd both sat up on instinct, looking toward the source of the noise.

And it was then that they'd seen it.

Mr. Markin, his body sprawled out on the asphalt, a red pool of blood circling his limp form. It was clear he was dead instantly. His chest didn't move, and something about the way his limbs were arranged spoke to his lack of life.

In front of him, the killer stood in plain view, still holding the shining silver handgun.

Janis remembered gasping for air, covering her mouth at the horror of it all. She had stood, rising to reach the cell phone she kept in her bag. She'd even managed to pull the phone out, but then— she'd risked a look at the murderer.

The killer had brought a hand to their lips: the universal sign for "shhh."

Without words, Janis knew what the murderer was threatening. She'd glanced over her shoulder at Sheila, half-naked on the couch. The killer knew them both personally, and was aware of what devastation revealing the affair would cause in both their lives. And, with a single gesture and a small smile, the killer had blackmailed them both into silence.

"It wouldn't matter anyway," Sheila had whispered, tears streaming down her face. "It's already done. It's already done." Janis remembered how small Sheila had looked at that moment, despite her lofty height.

"We should have called the police right then," Sheila said, snapping Janis back into the present moment as if she could see the memory replaying before them. "It was my fault. I told you not to call. I panicked—"

Janis didn't realize she was crying until she felt her nose run. She wiped it away as Sheila put an arm around her. "You're a better woman than I am."

"I just keep thinking that, if our places were reversed, Mr. Markin would have done the right thing. If it had been you or me out there, lying on the asphalt, he would have called."

"He would have," Sheila said.

"He was a good person," Janis added. "I haven't felt like a good person for a very long time. "

"But there's still time!" Sheila said. "We can change. From here on out, we make a deal," she held out a hand. "A life of honor and honesty. No more secrets. No more lies. From here on out, when we have the chance to do the right thing, we do it no matter how hard it is. For Mr. Markin."

Janis shook Sheila's hand, choosing to believe in the idea that she really could start all over.

"For Mr. Markin."

It had been torture, seeing the person who killed her neighbor still engaged in daily life at Aspen Lane. This person continued to masquerade as an upstanding member of the community, thinking they'd fooled the Detectives. But they hadn't. Annie was on to them. And, with her help, Janis was ready to tell the truth.

CHAPTER THIRTY-FOUR

JARED

JARED WAS in the middle of playing a video game when the local news story about Aspen Lane popped up in his feed. He was seated in front of his computer, which was attached to an expensive gaming console, controller in hand, virtual reality goggles covering his eyes. The notification came with a dinging sound that reminded Jared of a doorbell. It was a Pavlovian trigger he'd learned to ignore most of the time, but for some reason, this particular alert caught his attention. He removed his goggles just long enough to check the computer's feed, where the story appeared, along with a picture of Aspen Lane and Malcolm's face.

"Cover my right!" Edmonte shouted. He clicked at his controller, moving the virtual reality goggles he was wearing further up on his face. The shooting game involved military strategy, and all three brothers were supposed to participate as a team.

"I can't see you," Marcus added, always in last place. "Jared, get his right!"

Jared didn't answer. He was busy reading the news article, soaking up everything he could about Mr. Markin's case. Suddenly, he felt a hand on his shoulder. It was Edmonte, and Marcus behind him, both of them looking at Jared with heavy expressions.

"What?" Jared asked.

"You let us die out there man," Edmonte said. "And now you don't give a shit."

"It's a game," Jared shrugged.

"So it this," Edmonte pointed at the news article, then grabbed the mouse, closing the screen. "You were obsessed with the old man when he was alive, and you're still obsessed with him now."

"You don't know shit," Jared muttered, pushing his chair out from underneath the desk. "Mr. Markin actually cared about me as a person. All I am to you is a paycheck."

Edmonte stepped toward his brother, his face contorted with anger. "If that's what he made you believe, maybe it's good he's dead!"

Later, Jared would say he didn't remember doing it. But in a flash, he was on top of Edmonte, smacking him in the face and pulling him around the room, his brother's head locked in his arm, hands flailing.

"Don't you say shit about him!" Jared screamed, finally releasing Edmonte by pushing him into a wall. Edmonte seemed to cower, his brother Marcus standing next to him, the two of them staring at Jared like they were meeting him for the first time.

"I'm sorry," Jared said, hating himself once again. "I can't — I don't want to do the videos anymore." He let the information rest, wishing his brothers would tell him it was alright to give up. "It's over. All of it. It's done," he added, before turning on his heel and leaving the room.

CHAPTER THIRTY-FIVE

OTTO

OTTO DIDN'T CARE much for television. He found the obnoxious box to be too stimulating, with its blue-lit backscreen and constant modulations in volume. Otto preferred his books about the war when he was on security detail, and— when he wasn't reading one of those— he would occasionally turn on a podcast or the radio in the background of his car or house, just to make him feel less alone. He kept a small radio in the guard's booth at Aspen Lane for exactly such occasions, but tonight, Otto wasn't lonely. He didn't turn on the radio for company, even though his tiny guard booth did, at times, feel empty. Instead, Otto turned the radio on because he knew Aspen Lane was the centerpiece of an unfolding drama, and he couldn't afford to miss a single development.

Otto pushed his books aside, clearing stacks away to make room for the little black box. He leaned his back against the edge of the window in the guard's booth, giving his eyes some distance from the electronic readout that showed the radio's current channel. He scanned the stations, static and voices clicking, before finally stopping at a number he knew to be local news in Watersborough. Sure enough, the airwaves were rippling with a story about Aspen Lane.

"They're offering a reward for whoever finds the gun," a radio jockey with a baritone voice offered up. "Twenty grand. Hey Suzie, could you use some extra cash?"

"Not me," his female co-host's voice rang out into the night. "But something tells me Malcolm Havvendish could use the cash... to get a good lawyer!" A buzzing sound effect attempted to add a comic effect to the tasteless joke. Otto shook his head. People didn't take these things seriously enough. He hated the way the world made light of issues such as violence, war, love, and revenge.

Otto was familiar with all of the above. As a veteran who had spent extensive time in combat, he knew the dangers that lurked all around us. He understood that there were certain things worth dying for, and worth killing for. These clowns— the radio hosts— would never know such depth of feeling, because they existed as mere shadows of the human experience.

"To comment on the case," the radio host continued. "We have one of Watersborough's top defense attorneys in the studio. Ms. Reynolds, esquire. Thanks for stopping by."

"My pleasure," a woman's voice answered, the tenor of her tone an even shade of honey that was pleasing to the ear.

"So, what are their odds of making a case against Malcolm without the gun?"

"In today's world, forensics trumps everything," the lawyer said. "It's apparent from multiple sources they can prove a motive, given Malcolm Havvendish was listed as a major property recipient in Mr. Markin's will. But, as far as we know, there were no witnesses to the crime. A security guard heard the blast, and called 911—"

Otto felt his cheeks flush at the mention of his role in the investigation.

"—but he didn't witness anyone leaving the scene. This

means that to make their case a slam dunk, the District Attorney is going to have to present evidence that convinces the jury beyond a reasonable doubt. That's where the murder weapon comes in. Retrieving the weapon would help them trace the sequence of events. They can make the argument that Malcolm disposed of it as he fled the scene. Maybe even find some fingerprints. It cements the story. Makes an iron-clad case."

Otto listened to the report as if it were a bedtime story, glancing at the books on the built-in desk that sat in front of him, all of which were books on World War I and World War II. Otto preferred books that reflected on the tragedy of humanity— the way people so often sought to destroy rather than to build. Otto wished he could even the playing field so that the people that committed wrongs were held accountable, and the ones that did right were rewarded. But Otto was just a security guard, sitting in a small booth, at a cul-de-sac where nothing ever happened.

Nothing, until now.

CHAPTER THIRTY-SIX

FRANK

SINCE MALCOLM HAD BEEN ARRESTED, Frank and Lisa moved about their home as if in a waking dream. They made their breakfast. Cleaned the hardwood floors. They carried on with their lives as best they could, but all the while, concerns about their son floated in the background, begging for their attention. Late at night, Frank would page through internet search engines, looking for obscure laws he thought might help his son.

Tonight, Frank and Lisa were seated in front of the Television, two TV dinners propped up on plates, their eyes glued to the screen. Neither Frank nor Lisa had said it aloud, but they both knew what they were waiting for.

"Find anything new today?" Lisa asked, checking up on Frank's search for a legal loophole.

"Not today," Frank said. His fork hovered in the air, his hand unwilling to take another bite until the matter was resolved. "But it's only a matter of time. I'll keep reading—something will come up."

Lisa didn't answer, but looked at the full microwave dinner tray in front of her. Her appetite had disappeared with

Malcolm, and when she did eat, it was only to maintain the strength she needed to fight for her son.

"The lawyer we hired—"

"He's the best," Frank answered. They'd had this conversation again and again, going around in circles. It never led to anything except an argument.

"But maybe there's someone better—"

"It's going to take the man more than a few days to build a defense—"

Bubbling stock music from the television signaled the six o'clock local news had begun. Frank and Lisa fell into immediate silence, their eyes glued to the report. What had happened on Aspen Lane was the biggest story to hit Watersborough in years, and they knew any updates on the case would arrive first.

A female news anchor offered a traditional greeting before launching into the nightly news. A picture of Malcolm flashed above her head as an insert, just as Frank and Lisa knew it would.

"Tonight, Police are still asking for any information residents might have about a murder weapon used in the killing of a local man," the anchored said. "A suspect has been taken into custody—"

Frank cringed, as he always did when he heard his son described in such a fashion. Malcolm was not a suspect. Malcolm was a hero who had fought for his country. He was a brave man, who didn't deserve anything of this. Frank wanted to leap up at the TV, pull its cord from the wall outlet, and throw it across the room, watching the pieces blast with a satisfying electronic crunch. Instead, he sat in place, frozen, unable to make sense of how surreal this moment felt. It was as if someone had taken his life and turned it inside out, then handed it back to him with a smile. Nothing— absolutely nothing— made sense.

"Police believe the murder weapon may be a pivotal piece of the District Attorney's attempt to build an ironclad case," the anchor continued. "If you have any information, authorities urge you to call this number." A toll-free hotline number appeared on the screen.

Like clockwork, Frank and Lisa's cell phones began to buzz. Both phones were stacked on the fireplace mantle, purposefully out of sight. Frank stood, dragging himself toward the phones even though all he wanted to do was run away.

"We don't have to answer them," Lisa said.

Frank picked up both cell phones anyway and scrolled through the messages there. Whenever a story aired, they were bombarded by requests for comments. Journalists from around the greater Eastern Seaboard attempted to call, write, text message, and email both Frank and Lisa. But that wasn't what bothered Frank the most. What he hated most was the concerned reachouts from distant acquaintances. The text messages that said "How are you?" or "How's Malcolm holding up?" from people that had never been anything more than a distant connection. Suddenly, these so-called "friends of friends" thought it was appropriate to appear to care about Frank and Lisa when they'd never given a single damn about them before. Frank knew these people weren't interested in helping his family. All they wanted was to be a part of something bigger than themselves, at his expense. They wanted a taste of the drama so they could have a story to bring home to the dinner table, or to use at the next party they attended.

"Anything from her yet?" Lisa asked, watching Frank scroll through the phone.

"Not yet," Frank said. He set the phones back down on the mantle and returned to his seat, sinking into the couch. "But she'll call when she has something. She promised she would."

The fact of the matter was that Frank and Lisa's phones

had been ringing since all of this happened. But there was only one person in the world they were eager to hear from. One woman who held their son's fate in her hands:

Detective Annie Hudson.

CHAPTER THIRTY-SEVEN

ANNIE AND ETHAN were at their new favorite diner, enjoying cheeseburgers soaked in grease when they got the call. They'd been watching a live news feed on the case, broadcast on the diner's wall-mounted television. Waitresses in red aprons scooted by, occasionally blocking the screen from view. Each time his line of sight was blocked, Ethan would crane his neck around the passing figure so as not to miss a single piece of the story being broadcast overhead. In contrast, Annie took calm, determined bites out of her burger, treating the ongoing broadcast as if it were a simple story about the weather.

"You're going to hurt your neck if you keep craning like that," Annie said, motioning to Ethan's posture as the waitress passed yet again.

"It's been three days," Ethan answered. "Even the national news has picked it up. Three days, and no gun."

"It will come," Annie said, unaffected. "A watched pot never boils."

Ethan forced himself to look away from the screen, turning his attention to the plate in front of him. His burger sat there, untouched and getting cold. "This is a lot, Annie," he said. He ran a hand through his hair, and the tousled effect didn't go unnoticed by Annie, who tried to suppress the feeling she sometimes had around him. "It reminds me of when the stories about my sister and your brother were everywhere. I could walk down the street without seeing her face in a newspaper. Couldn't go to the grocery store without running into a missing poster."

Annie reached across the table and touched his hand. She understood. She had seen the image of her brother— murdered in cold blood— circulated throughout the news cycle like it was nothing but another story. And it was... to everyone else. But to Annie, it was a traumatic reminder. An image she could never unsee. She hated to do this to Malcolm's parents, but it was the only way to assure his future.

"We're flushing the real killer out. There's no other way Trust me. If we play this right, Malcolm will go free."

The way Ethan crinkled the corners of his eyes told Annie he had doubts about their plan. She needed Ethan on her team and was about to reassure him when his phone buzzed.

Ethan and Annie glanced at each other, and Annie's pulse quickened with the sweet intensity that told her she was close to breaking a case. Ethan grabbed his phone, reading a message that appeared on the screen.

"Well?" Annie prompted.

Ethan looked up in disbelief. "You were right," he said. "They found the gun."

Annie crumpled her napkin into a ball, then rose from the booth, ready to complete this investigation and return Aspen Lane to a new normal. "Next lunch is on you," she smiled at Ethan, dropping cash on the table. They headed for the double glass doors that marked the entrance to the diner, and Ethan got the sense that this case was almost closed, and they might be one step closer to leaving Watersborough for good, never returning to those fraying, plastic booths.

Suddenly hungry, he murmured under his breath, "I should've eaten my burger."

CHAPTER THIRTY-EIGHT

ETHAN'S unmarked van curled its way down a narrow side road that backed up to an embankment. Overgrown chaparral reached across the edge of the riverbank, tendrils of dry branches landing on the asphalt road. To Annie, it looked as if the trees were attempting to escape the creek. It was as if they knew this was a place better left alone.

The car door slammed as Annie and Ethan emerged from within, walking toward a collection of parked police cruisers, their lights flashing. Chief Hardgrave clocked their arrival and strode to meet them, a blue windbreaker tight around her shoulders.

"We've gotta a positive I.D.," she said, skipping the greetings. "The gun matches the bullet that forensics found in our victim." She motioned for Ethan and Annie to follow her, then flagged down another officer, who was holding a plastic bag. Hardgrave retrieved the bag, lifting it so Annie and Ethan could evaluate its contents. Within was a silver handgun, shining under the moonlight. "A Colt 1911," Hardgrave said. "We ran registration. It belongs to one Mr. Malcolm Havvendish."

"This riverbank," Annie said, ignoring the gun. "It backs up to Aspen Lane..."

"To the Eastern side," Hardgrave confirmed. "Runs right behind Malcolm Havvendish's house."

"But the entire street is enclosed by an iron fence," Annie said. "It attaches to the gates and continues off from there. Which side of the embankment was the gun found on?"

"Our officers found it street side," Hardgrave said.

Annie moved toward the embankment, evaluating the geography of the river. It was about twenty feet wide, and on the far end, backed up to the public road. The river itself was low this time of year, better described as a creek. It was a small outlet for a channel of water that only spanned a three-foot width. Without warning, Annie lowered herself down the embankment, heading for the water.

"Annie?" Ethan called behind her, but she was already on the move. She stepped into the river, finding that the water only came to her knees. Her legs shook from the cold as she waded across the channel, and in a few steps, arrived safely at the other side. She hauled herself out of the water, stepping with ease onto the incline at the other side. A quick scramble of hands and legs led her to the top, where she grabbed the root of a tree to pull her upward. She was on the other end, now, facing a line of trees that backed up to something man-made. Annie reached through a tangle of branches, closing her hand around a pole that belonged to the iron fence that circled Aspen Lane.

"That's Malcom's house," Hardgrave called over the distance. "Backs right up to it." Annie pulled the branches apart, looking through the slats in the fence to the backyard within. Behind it was a house that Annie recognized as belonging to Frank, Lisa, and Malcolm. She had seat it from the opposite point of view just recently, when she'd been a guest in their living room.

Annie took a single deep breath as if she were allowing

her conclusion to simmer within her lungs, a recipe cooking to completion. Then, she slid back down the embankment, finding Ethan standing in the water, one hand reaching out, waiting for her.

"Madame," he said. Annie rolled her eyes, but let him help her across the creek. Together, they hiked back up the street side of the embankment, presenting themselves to Hardgrave like a pair of shivering dogs.

"Matthews!" Hardgrave shouted at another office. "Get us a couple of blankets over here?"

The officer disappeared into the back of a squad car, returning with two foil blankets, which he handed to Annie and Ethan.

"It wasn't Malcolm," Annie said. She took a seat on the hood of a squad car, wrapping the blanket around her wet jeans. "To dispose of the gun from *inside* Aspen Lane, he would have had to have run to his backyard, then throw the gun *over* a twelve-foot fence, thirty feet across the embankment. It's just not possible," Annie added, teeth chattering. Ethan ran a hand over her back, trying to warm her up. "Whoever dropped that gun dropped it from the street. They drove down this road, which almost nobody knows about."

"It's hard to see from the main street," Ethan agreed.

"Which tells us they're a local to the neighborhood," Annie said. "Everyone who lives at Aspen Lane would know this tributary backs up to the property. Someone *knew* this particular spot backed up to Malcolm's house, and they drove up that road, dropping the gun street side."

Chief Hardgrave let out a low whistle like she hated to admit what she was about to say. "Believe it or not, I agree with you," she confirmed. "When the murder was reported, our cadets searched this place from top to bottom. If the gun had been in the river, they would have found it. This was newly placed in plain sight, not a single branch or leaf covering it from view. It looked like it was planted by somebody who wanted to make sure we'd see it," Hardgrave continued. "Not to mention Malcolm would have to be fucking stupid to toss the gun by his own house."

"Was it loaded?" Annie asked.

"Five rounds," Hardgrave confirmed.

"Malcolm served in the military," Annie added. "He was a pistol champion. He'd know better than to toss a loaded gun that way."

"Still, I'm 'gonna need more to make a new arrest," Hardgrave leaned against a squad car. "And it better be fucking right this time."

"It will be," Annie said. "If you trust me," she paused a beat, considering. "How was the gun reported?"

"Anonymous call," Hardgrave nodded, agreeing with Annie's conclusion before she offered it. "Made from a public phone down on Main Street. Suspicious, I know," she clocked Annie's facial expression. "What person that stands to gain a twenty-thousand dollar reward decides to provide the information anonymously? I'm with you, Annie," she said, the words feeling wrong as they rolled around her mouth. "Where do we go from here?"

"I believe," Annie smiled. "It's time for one, final neighborhood meeting. But first, I need to make a quick pit stop."

"Where?" Ethan asked.

There was a long pause, then, Annie offered an answer Ethan hadn't expected. "To the guard booth at Aspen Lane."

CHAPTER THIRTY-NINE

FOR THE SAKE OF POETRY, Annie chose to end the thing where it began. After sending officers to knock on every door, Annie and Ethan assembled the neighbors in the middle of the cul-de-sac at Aspen Lane, each of them concerned about this new development. Krystal stood with a shawl wrapped around her shoulders, silver bangles clinging to its fringe. Jared and his two brothers arranged themselves in a kind of triangle toward the back of the group, with Edmonte and Marcus standing a little separate from their brother as if they were afraid of being declared guilty by association. Janis and Sheila were side-by-side, the latter still shaking dried clay from her hands. She'd been in her pottery studio when she'd seen all the commotion, but this time was actually making something other than love to Janis. Reggie and Melissa were at opposite ends of the group, both of them looking lonely and a little out of place. Finally, Otto paced behind Annie and Ethan, looking at each resident as if they might be the guilty party and blocking the exit so they couldn't make a run for it. Annie had asked him to provide security at the gathering— a matter which he took rather seriously.

"We've gathered you here," Annie stated, "to offer a conclusion as to the matter of who killed Mr. Markin. I'll cut to the point. The murderer is among us."

Mutters flittered through the group as everyone looked to their left and right. The neighbors knew each other well enough to have grievances. But they'd always mutually considered these issues to be ones of a pettier nature. Never did they think they'd be trying to identify a murderer in their midst. There was a moment of silence, then Krystal spoke first.

"Nobody here would have hurt Mr. Markin. We might not always get along, but—"

"We're neighbors," Reggie finished her sentence. "I can't stand half these people and some of them can't stand me, but we don't kill each other over it. We're not that *kind* of neighborhood."

Just then, there was a squeaking sound as the iron gates opened. Otto turned, surprised to see the gates operating on their own. Behind him, a brigade of Police Cruisers made their way into the cul-de-sac, forming a barricade to exit.

"Hope you don't mind, Otto," Annie said, all smiles. "But the FBI made a call to the gate company and took over the reins. Still need you on security, though."

"Not a problem," Otto said, the look in his eye indicating it was *very* much a problem. But for now, he chose to ignore it, given the importance of his role in these proceedings.

"Just one more guest," Annie motioned to the first police car. Officer Hardgrave emerged from the driver's side, opening the back door to reveal a figure within. Malcolm stepped out of the car, Frank and Lisa by his side. The family made their way toward the rest of the neighbors, a breezy quality marking their steps. Malcolm's expression betrayed nothing, except that he looked a little worse for wear, a patchy scruff of a beard growing on his chin.

"How are you holding up, Malcolm?" Annie asked.

"Just fine, Annie," he lied, giving her a thumbs up. His wrists were free, unencumbered by the handcuffs that had previously been restricting his movement. He took his place in the group of neighbors, Frank and Lisa by his side.

"Now that the entire street is here, we'll begin," Annie said. "Whether you know it or not, each and every one of you played an integral role in this case, mostly through unintentional lies and subterfuge."

"*Excuse* me?" Melissa started to say before Ethan shushed her.

"Not because all of you were guilty of this particular crime, but because of the culture here in Watersborough. Never in my life have I seen a community so concerned with appearance."

"Like, tell me about it," Krystal admitted under her breath.

"If any one of you had cared more about bringing justice to Mr. Markin than you did about protecting your own reputation, this case might have been solved much more quickly, and poor Malcolm wouldn't have been made to suffer."

Guilty looks among the group shot toward Malcolm, who didn't move an inch.

"If any *one* of you had been less self-absorbed, you might have heard the gunshot in the first place, and there would be no mystery to solve at all. It's ironic, that Malcolm took the blame, seeing as this all began with him anyway."

"How?" Frank asked. He was relieved to have his son back but still afraid of where Annie's investigation would go.

"Malcolm doesn't like noise," Annie answered. "In fact, noise brings Malcolm back to the battlefield. Having been diagnosed with PTSD, Malcolm came to his parents' house, just hoping for a little peace. A goal all of *you*—" Annie pointed around the circle, "— made utterly impossible."

"PTSD?" Sheila gasped, horrified. "The garage conversion. Frank, is that why—"

"It is," Frank answered. "When Reggie came to me and

wanted to fight you on it, I agreed because I knew the noise would make it harder on Malcolm. It's not that I didn't want you to have your studio—"

"I could've done without," Sheila answered quickly. "Malcolm, why didn't you bloody say something?"

"I can handle it," Malcolm shrugged. "Didn't want anyone to have to change their lives around on account of me."

"Our parties," Jared said. "If we'd known, we wouldn't have been so loud—"

"But you *did* know," Annie said. "Not about Malcolm but about the way the neighborhood felt about your weekend raves. The cops were called multiple times. Noise complaint after noise complaint. And the three of you continued despite it all, so caught up in your selfish world that you had no idea a veteran was struggling down the street from you. But then again," Annie paced, loving the way it felt to piece the puzzle together. "I can hardly single you out. Every person on this street was so self-absorbed that they didn't look to their left or their right. Don't you see?" Annie paused, for effect. "You miss each other. You drive past one another every day. But you don't *see* each other."

The neighbors looked at the ground, each of them feeling the weight of her words.

"The only person who *did* see his neighbors was Mr. Markin," Annie said. She stopped her pacing, standing in place before the group. "He saw every single one of you. He tried to help you move past your struggles. Starting with you," she pointed at Jared. "Mr. Markin saw in you a younger version of himself. A lost young man, trying to run away from his mistakes but unable to overcome them on his own."

"He was trying to help me get clean," Jared admitted to the group. The neighbors shifted, uncomfortable. Watersborough wasn't a place where addiction was discussed out in the open. "I'm addicted to painkillers. He was trying to help me get sober."

Edmonte and Marcus exchanged shocked glances. "You never—" Edmonte stuttered, suddenly worried for his brother. "You didn't tell me. We could have stopped—"

"Mr. Markin noticed the people around him," Annie continued, "and that's why he saw that Jared needed help. He befriended him, building trust. Which brings us to the robbery the week before the murder. At first, it seemed the two events must be connected. The occurrence of the robbery so close to the murder presented a false distraction, unintentionally caused by someone Mr. Markin cared for."

"It was me," Jared answered. Everyone stared. "I broke into Mr. Markin's house. I left drugs there and I went back to get them. I took the vase to make it look like a robbery but it wasn't. It was just me, taking back what I'd left."

"The lawn furniture that day!" Reggie exclaimed, turning to Jared. "Did you tip over my set to cover your tracks? You know that set was custom ordered—"

"Actually, that was me," Janis raised a hand. "Well, not me alone, but Sheila was over and—"

"I like the sunshine on my skin," Sheila shrugged. "It's an Australian thing."

"You came home early," Janis said to Reggie, "So we didn't have time to put the furniture back."

Reggie pulled at his hair, at his wit's end with the entire charade. "Are there *any* other injustices I have to endure—"

"Jared was responsible for robbing Mr. Markin," Annie continued. "The robbery created the perfect opportunity for the killer to strike. You see, the murderer had been waiting for some time. This person had been researching Mr. Markin's habits. The killer treated this exercise like a plot in a book, looking to intentionally tangle the threads in the hopes of confusing law enforcement. The robbery offered a perfect cover. One week later, the killer would strike." Annie paused, then added, "But let's rewind. Jared wasn't the only young man Mr. Markin was mentoring. Six months earlier, he had met and assisted Frank and Lisa's son, Malcolm, who had just moved home."

"It's true," Malcolm turned to the group. "Mr. Markin was my friend."

"Mr. Markin was the only one on the street besides Frank and Lisa who knew what Malcolm was going through. And he took Malcolm to a special event. Malcolm?"

"It was a squadron reunion," Malcolm said. "He took me to meet the guys he served with in Vietnam. He hadn't seen some of them in fifty years."

"And there it is," Annie exclaimed, throwing a finger in the air so sharply it caused the rest of the group to jump up in alarm. "The key to understanding Mr. Markin. When I heard Malcolm's story, I wondered how I could have missed it. Mr. Markin did so many acts of kindness for the community. He acted with such grace that it almost looked like a man atoning for something. Because he *was* atoning for something."

Annie shot a pointed glance at Malcolm, who swallowed hard. It felt wrong to betray Mr. Markin, but to bring his killer to justice, it was necessary to reveal the truth.

"Mr. Markin was young when he was drafted," Malcolm said. "Like, nineteen. He was still a kid. He told me— he told me he made a huge mistake out there. He was with a few other soldiers in his squadron and they were getting hit hard. He left them. Abandoned his fellow men out there. They were captured, and he could never let it go. He promised to do good from there on out. But still, it haunted him the rest of his life."

"So much so," Annie said, " that he never attended a single squadron reunion. Until he met Malcolm and found some sort of healing. He was willing to face his fears and attend the reunion, so long as it meant helping Malcolm." Annie turned to Malcolm, looking him dead in the eye. "You helped heal him," she said. "I hope you know that."

"What does all this have to do with the murder?" Reggie asked, eager to get to the point.

"Of course," Annie said. "Let's fast-forward in time, bringing us to the evening Mr. Markin was killed. I asked myself, 'Why would the killer lure him into the middle of the street?' Wouldn't it have been simpler just to shoot Mr. Markin in his own home? But then it occurred to me that Mr. Markin was already out in the road, even at such a late hour, because he was intending to go somewhere on foot. Given the angle his body was at and the fact that he was shot through his left pectoral muscle, it looked as if Mr. Markin was simply crossing the street. Which means the killer didn't lure him out at all. The killer simply waited for the opportunity and took it."

"But where would he have been going?" Lisa asked, relieved that the trail of revelations seemed to be leading away from Malcolm.

"Krystal?" Annie said gently, taking a step forward.

Krystal looked around the cul-de-sac like there might be another version of her somewhere. "Who? Me?"

"Do you want to share with the group why Mr. Markin was crossing the street that night?"

Krystal shook her head. Tears welled up in her eyes.

"Come on," Jared urged. "I already admitted I'm an addict and a robber. How much worse can yours be?"

"You were giving Mr. Markin free readings," Annie pushed.

"Because I owed him," Krystal said, her lower lip trembling. "I wanted to expand the business with branded merchandise and an online store. I got— I got Mr. Markin to agree to invest. But I swear I thought it would work this time!" She added.

"*This* time?" Melissa scoffed.

"The business had been doing so much better here than in California. Less competition I guess. And no matter what you all believe," Krystal pointed a finger at the group, "I *am* a real psychic. I'm just bad at numbers! And the cards told me it would work this time. But then the money ran out and—"

"And you stopped taking Mr. Markin's calls?"

Krystal nodded. "He called me that night," she added, tears spilling over her cheeks. "Maybe ten times. I know he wanted me to start paying on the loan he gave me so he could do other things with the money, but I didn't have anything to give him. It all just went away so quick—"

"Did you hear the gunshot that night?"

"Yes," Krystal said. "But I didn't know it was a gunshot. All I knew was Mr. Markin had called me five minutes earlier. He left a voicemail saying he needed to talk and if I didn't answer he was going to come knock on my door. I think—" her voice quivered. "I think he was having trouble sleeping because what I'd done bothered him so much."

"Not because of the money," Annie clarified. "But because you wouldn't take accountability for what had happened with it."

"I heard the bang outside, but didn't dare open my curtains," Krystal said. "It wasn't until later when the cop cars came that I pieced it all together."

"And you destroyed the evidence of your agreement?" Annie asked, even though she already knew the answer.

"I— went to his hou-house," Krystal was sobbing, now. "Aa- and burned all the paperwork." She wiped the tears away. "I've always been bad at keeping track of money, but I've never done anything like that. I was just so scared that they'd blame me. Or that it would all come out, and—"

"And you'd lose your standing in the community," Annie said. "Typical, of this street it seems. And on that thread, it occurred to me that the odds of not a single person in this quiet enclave hearing the sound of a gunshot were minuscule. Five homes, besides Mr. Markin, and I was expected to believe that not a single person heard the shot? Ethan, does that sound plausible to you?"

"No, ma'am," Ethan answered. He always enjoyed this part.

"But of course, as we now know, somebody *did* hear the shot. Krystal. And two *other* people who were awake at that time." Annie paused, fixing her attention on Janis and Sheila. "Janis?"

Janis was already crying. It seemed, since the night of Mr. Markin's murder, all she'd done was cry. "Sheila and I saw it," Janis said. "We saw it because—"

"Because they're having an *affair,*" Reggie said for her. The neighbors gasped.

"That wasn't your story to tell!" Sheila shouted at him.

"Sure as hell felt like my story, since it happened to *me,"* Regie answered.

Janis continued with her confession before the two of them could escalate the argument. "Sheila and I were— we were having an intimate moment in the pottery studio the night Mr. Markin was killed. It was so late we didn't think anyone would be out. We— forgot to close the curtains. And those big windows in the studio, they look right out at the street. You can see the entire cul-de-sac."

"A perfect line of sight," Annie confirmed.

"We heard the bang. It was so loud at first that I thought it was a firecracker, but then when I looked out the window, I saw it. Mr. Markin was lying on the ground. And the killer was standing over him, holding the gun. I wanted to call the police but—"

"You couldn't," Annie finished Janis's sentence for her. "Because the killer blackmailed you. With one simple gesture." Annie brought her finger to her lips in the universal sign for "shh," mimicking what the killer had done. "You knew this person had the power to out you to everyone. To destroy your reputation. So you kept quiet. Well," Annie paused, smiling. "Not totally quiet." She paced again, carving paths across the asphalt. "When we began this exercise, I told you all we had three mysteries to solve. The robbery, which has now been closed, thanks to Jared. The murder, which we are just beginning to unravel. And, finally, the issue of my hiring. Whoever sent me that letter knew about the murder before the FBI. They hired me anonymously."

"It was me," Janis answered. "I couldn't sleep that night and felt so awful. I hired you. I had a courier express ship the envelope with your fee enclosed. It cost a fortune but I didn't care. I figured if you could get to the bottom of it without involving Sheila and me, maybe Mr. Markin would get his justice."

"Yes," Annie agreed. "It would be wonderful if such a thing were possible. But sadly, an eyewitness account means the world to a jury. And so, Janis? Sheila? Would you like to tell us who you saw standing over Mr. Markin's body that night?"

Janis and Sheila looked at each other, then, in unison, raised their hands to point not at Annie, but at a figure behind her.

"Otto," Janis said. There was an edge to her voice, like she'd been carrying his name around in her mouth since the event had occurred and was finally glad to be rid of it. "Otto killed Mr. Markin."

All eyes turned to Otto, who had— during this conversation— been scanning the police barricade for any exit. Finding none, he had moved himself to the fringe of the group, as if he was hoping to go unnoticed. He stared back at the group, his mouth wide with shock.

"Me?" Otto laughed. "You can't be serious. You have no evidence. He's the one with the motivation—" Otto pointed at Malcolm. "Why would I want Mr. Markin dead?"

"Ah, yes, a lucky strike for you, that Malcolm happened to

be named in Mr. Markin's will. You didn't know the perfect cover would land in your lap when you stole the gun from Malcolm's house. You only hoped using one of his weapons would convince the police the blame lay elsewhere. You spoke to the neighbors frequently and knew Malcolm was a pistol champ. So you broke into Frank and Lisa's basement—easily accessed from the faulty basement window in the backyard." She glanced at Lisa and Frank. "I told you, very dangerous to leave these things open." The couple blinked, the reality of what had happened dawning on them. Annie focused back on Otto. "You waited until they were out of the house, then broke in and raided Malcolm's gun collection, taking the Colt 1911. I assume you chose it for the symbolic meaning behind it, no?"

Otto didn't answer. Annie turned back to the group, explaining. "The Colt 1911 was the standard issue handgun during Vietnam. A war which Otto fought in, isn't that correct, Otto?"

"Fought in?" Otto scoffed. "More like went to die in. You have no idea what it takes out there."

"I do," Malcolm said. "It takes honor, something you don't have—"

"Otto was part of Mr. Markin's squadron in Vietnam, but not just any part," Annie continued. "Otto was one of the men Mr. Markin left behind. One of the ones that were captured and— as Mr. Markin incorrectly assumed— ultimately killed in enemy hands. But you *weren't* killed, were you Otto? You made it out alive. And you never forgot what happened to you."

"Damn right, I never forgot!" Otto yelled, his voice a seething volcano in the middle of the otherwise quiet street. "The look on the bastard's face when he ran! He had a chance to fight. To save his brothers, or to go down together. The coward left us." He moved closer to Annie, almost nose-to-nose with her. "You ever been in a prison camp? Any idea what it's like to be a prisoner of war? Torture. Starvation. But I survived. Because I had a purpose. I promised I'd take back my power."

"But when you got out, you couldn't find him," Annie said. "Because Mr. Markin had removed himself from every possible database. He wanted to forget the war and forget what he'd done and put the past behind him. In an unexpected way, his shame and his guilt protected him. Until..."

"Until he took me to the squadron reunion," Malcolm said, horror crossing his face. "We all took a photo together. They put it up on the website."

"Yes," Annie said. "A quick internet search showed us that the picture was posted front and center on the reunion group's website," she turned to Otto. "And that's where you recognized the man who'd left you behind. From there, it wasn't hard to figure out where he lived. You'd already been employed as a security guard, and your military background made passing their rigorous hiring requirements a simple task. You took the job at Aspen Lane and waited. You watched his every move. You planned the crime. And when the robbery happened, you knew you had finally found the brief window you'd been looking for — your opportunity to get even with Mr. Markin once and for all."

"This is a lovely theory," Otto snarled. "But the murder weapon belongs to *him,"* he pointed at Malcolm. "Good luck convincing a jury I had anything to do with it."

"Yes," Annie nodded. "My favorite part. I asked myself... what was the murderer doing with the gun after the killing? Why not just dispose of it? Of course, it was because you didn't have time. After you shot Mr. Markin, you headed straight back to the guard's booth, where you needed to make the 911 call as soon as possible. You needed to hide the gun somewhere in the booth nobody else would think to look, just long enough to stash it and avoid detection." Annie glanced at Police Chief Hardgrave, who motioned at another officer stationed by Otto's guard booth.

"Bring it here," Hardgrave said. The officer emerged from the booth, a single book in hand. At the sight of the book, the blood rushed from Otto's face.

"Do you want to do the honors or should I?" Annie asked, taking the book from the officer and smiling at Otto. "I'll do it," she said, flipping open the front cover. There, in the pages, was a cut-away space that created a small compartment. The paper had been skillfully removed in a particular shape that made no change to the book's exterior but allowed the owner to hide something within. "Ethan?" Annie asked.

Ethan pulled the plastic bag containing the gun from his jacket pocket. Carefully not to touch the gun itself, he used the bag as a glove, turning it inside out and dumping the gun into the cutout in the book.

"A perfect fit," Annie said. "After killing Mr. Markin, Otto ran back to his security booth and stashed the gun in one of his many books, which he knew the police would never bother to examine. Later, when he heard our false report that the gun was a key piece of evidence in building a case against Malcolm, he drove down the backroad street adjacent to the river, and tossed it on the embankment near Malcolm's house." Annie turned to Otto, shaking her head. "Clever, except that you chose the street side of the river, not the side closest to the gates. That was really where you went wrong. Nothing to be ashamed of. Everyone ends up incriminating themselves somehow." Annie clapped her hands together, very pleased with what she'd accomplished. "And there it is! All three pieces of the mystery solved. Satisfying, isn't it?"

What happened next came to fruition with such ferocity, that the neighbors would later say time seemed to slow down, as if life had become a slow-motion movie. In a single swoop, Otto pushed the officer standing next to him aside, wrestling the gun from his holster. Concerned for no one but

Annie, Ethan pulled her behind him, positioning himself in front of her so that his entire body covered her own. Officer Hardgrave leaped forward, drawing her gun, but it was too late. Otto already had his hands on the weapon, pointing it at Ethan, Annie, and the neighbors, flicking off the safety with the hand of a practiced expert.

"Very satisfying," Otto said, his finger tight on the trigger.

CHAPTER FORTY

"A WONDERFUL TWIST," Annie said. Ethan still stood in front of her, shielding her body with his own. Otto held the gun level, looking for any openings that might allow him an escape route. A nervous energy rippled through the neighbors, and a few— acting on instinct— even threw their hands into the air, as if to signal they meant no harm. The brigade of officers blocking the exit all had their guns drawn, a dozen fatal barrels pointed at Otto.

"I'll be so curious to see how this ends," Annie continued. Her tone was genuine, and she appeared unaffected by the threat in front of her. Where everyone else on Aspen Lane was holding their breath— fearful of being injured should the standoff lead to a shootout— Annie was calm. She treated this moment as if it were just another moment among many. Nothing special about it. Perhaps it was because her nightmares frightened her more than anything the real world could ever again throw at her.

"Stay behind me," Ethan said to Annie, pushing her further back.

"Drop the gun!" Hardgrave shouted, moving closer with

her weapon in hand. "You're surrounded, Otto. There's nowhere to go from here."

Otto's eyes scanned the scene, trying to puzzle his way out. The collective of officers still blocked the exit, and the iron gates to the cul-de-sac were shut. There was no way he could make a break for it, unless, perhaps, he tried to take a hostage. Even then, he risked being killed by a sniper shot sent from the right angle. There had to be a way out. Otto chewed on the problem, and when no answer arrived, he set his eyes on Annie, a new determination there. "Maybe I'm going down," he said. "But it doesn't mean I can't take her with me."

Otto's finger pulled tighter on the trigger, but then, a small miracle descended on the group. A voice rang out from the back of the collective of neighbors.

"You'll have to take me first," Frank said. He stepped forward, striding toward Annie, joining Ethan in standing in front of her.

"And me," his wife Lisa's voice rang out behind him. She ran toward Frank, wrapping her arms around him.

"Me, too," Malcolm said. He stood beside his mother and father, taking his Mom's hand in his. The three of them created a human blockade around Annie and Ethan, shielding them from Otto's next move.

"And like, I guess me also," Krystal said. She looked surprised to hear her own voice joining the fray, but then, a steely resolve crossed her face. Her stiletto heels clicked across the asphalt as she positioned herself next to Malcolm. "I let Mr. Markin down," she said, voice quaking. "But the least I can do to honor his memory is try to be better, from here on out."

"That's what Mr. Markin did," Janis said, pushing her way through the other neighbors. "He made a mistake, but he dedicated the rest of his life to fixing it." She strode across the cul-de-sac, standing next to Krystal, adding herself to the growing human fence that protected Annie and Ethan. "I've made some really big mistakes lately," she glanced at Reggie, something unspoken exchanged between the two of them. "But I intend to do better, going forward. I should've called the police the second I saw you standing over his body, you pathetic, sick fuck," she said straight to Otto. "I've spent so much of my life being afraid, and I let Mr. Markin down. But I won't let Annie down. If you want her, you'll have to take me first."

"And if you want *her,*" Sheila said, stepping in front of Janis. "You'll have to go through me."

"And me," Jared said. He joined the group in front of Annie, Edmonte and Marcus keeping pace behind him. "Mr. Markin taught us that neighbors help each other. So, if you want to hurt anyone here, you'll have to go through us." At his heels, Marcus and Edmonte nodded, with Edmonte pounding a fist into his hand.

"You might be quick with that trigger, man," Edmonte said. "But there's more of us than there are of you."

"Many more," Reggie said. He joined the circle, Melissa by his side. Now, the blockade around Annie was complete, with every neighbor creating a protective shield around her and Ethan. "I may not like everyone that lives on this street," Reggie said. "But I've learned I can be wrong about people," he glanced at Melissa, who was now, undeniably, his friend.

Melissa glared at Otto, pushing her glasses higher on her face. "It's not you that protects Aspen Lane, or those stupid gates." She nodded at the weaving iron entryway that had—for so long— given them a sense of security. "It's *us* that makes this street special. All of us. Mr. Markin saw that. He was a good neighbor. And you're going to answer for what you did to him."

Melissa clasped hands with Reggie, who took the hand of the person next to him. who took the hand of the next person, and suddenly the whole neighborhood was standing there, united, forming an impenetrable barrier that Otto could not cross. From behind the safety of their interlocked fingers, Annie couldn't help but notice that the united neighbors looked something like the iron gates in front of them. Each person reminded her of a bar in the protective structure, their varying heights mimicking the way the top of the security gates seemed to slop in height.

There was a breathless moment in which everyone waited for a shot to ring out, but the sound never came. All at once, Otto dropped the gun. He slumped to the ground, crouched on his heels. He let his head fall into his hands, momentarily projecting himself to some other place or some other time. Nobody could say where he went, but the wailing sounds that choked from his mouth said it was a place he didn't want to be.

Annie stepped around the collective, heading toward Otto. The police rushed forward, seizing the opportunity to make their arrest. Hardgrave removed handcuffs from her belt, snapping them on Otto's wrists. "You have the right to remain silent," she said, beginning the Miranda rights. Annie kicked the gun away from Otto, then crouched beside him. She put a hand on his back, rubbing it in a circular movement, her pacing matching Otto's as Hardgrave pushed him toward the police car. Otto gave the impression of an inconsolable animal, his guttural cries still filling the air. Annie whispered something to him, and it seemed to calm him down for a moment. He looked at her, something gentle in his eyes, and then he was pushed into the police car, and the moment was gone.

The neighbors hugged each other, the petty fights of the past a distant memory. Annie returned to the group, leaning on Ethan, completely unaffected by what had just happened.

Krystal laughed at Annie's loping demeanor. "Weren't you, guys like, scared?" she said.

"I was terrified," Ethan joked. "Except that I'm used to it.

It's not the first time this one's put me in the line of fire," he winked at Annie.

"I wasn't scared," Annie took in the neighbors, noticing how— for the first time— they appeared as friends instead of distant strangers living separate lives next door to one another. "After all, I was with all of you."

She smiled at the group, knowing without a doubt that Aspen Lane would never see such trouble again. Even in death, Mr. Markin had changed these people, using the light of his own kindness to spark the same fire in another person. These disparate neighbors might have been broken as individuals, but together, they built a more complete, operational whole. *How poetic it is,* Annie thought to herself, that right here on the asphalt, dead-center in the middle of the street, a new start was proffered in the place where it all began.

The idea was more than a suspicion. It was a clear fact to Annie, and a beautiful truth:

In the place where Mr. Markin had died, the neighborhood had been reborn.

CHAPTER FORTY-ONE

THE BUSINESS of wrapping up the case was straightforward and clinical. There was paperwork to be filed. There were attorneys to be named. There were press interviews to be arranged. Annie and Ethan quickly turned it all over to the Watersborough Police Department and Chief Hardgrave, who was more than happy to collect the credit for bringing Otto into custody.

Ethan prepared his brief for the FBI, disappointed that he had to share his finding that this case did not relate to the serial murderer known as the Real Estate Ripper. There were a few at the Bureau who knew his personal connection to the crime but generally, Ethan tried to downplay his very deep need to see justice served, lest it lead to accusations of clouded vision and bias. He knew what awaited him— a string of other cases that threatened the nation's security. He also knew that all of them would feel a little hollow, without Annie by his side. He would return to his pattern of waiting, hoping for something to appear that would give him an excuse to bring her on as a consultant. Until then, he would just— *miss* her.

Finally, it was time to leave Watersborough. Annie and

Ethan went to get lunch at their new favorite diner— a tribute to another case closed.

"This time I'm eating my burger," Ethan said, taking a huge bite of the cheeseburger he was holding.

Annie shifted in her plastic seat, looking a little dismayed. On the TV overhead, a news story about Otto's pending trial date played, Chief Hardgrave front and center before a line of reporters.

"Something got you down?" Ethan asked, mouth full.

"I thought this was connected," Annie said. "The way the letter arrived. It was exactly three words. The style of the handwriting was even similar."

"Suspicions aren't facts," Ethan quoted Annie's favorite line back at her.

"True," Annie admitted. "But my suspicions often turn out to be right." She took a sip of her milkshake. "Maybe I'm just sad I won't have an excuse to see *you* and that's what's got me down."

"You can see me anytime you want," Ethan told her. "If you'd just take my referral and join the FBI."

"Can't," Annie told him, as she had many times before. "I'm a lone operative."

"You'd be great, Annie," Ethan continued. "It's a real family there. Lots of bureaucratic bullshit but more autonomy than you'd think. You have such a mind for it."

"I'll think about it," Annie said, both of them knowing she wouldn't.

"I'd get to see you every day," Ethan added. "That's a selling point, right?"

"A huge one," Annie admitted. She'd never let herself enter into a permanent connection with Ethan, because— if Annie was being honest— she was afraid to get too close to anyone. Getting close to people meant having something to lose, and Annie? She'd lost enough.

She thought about the way Ethan had stood in front of

her, staring down the barrel of Otto's gun like he was willing to die for her. It was rare, to find such a partner. This investigation had deepened something between them, and there was no going back from that. Annie stood. She moved to Ethan's side of the booth, scooting in close to him. He naturally put his arm around her, and she let him. He looked at her, a little surprised.

"Let's not make a big thing out of it," she said, taking a bite of his cheeseburger.

"Wasn't going to," Ethan smiled.

Just then, a familiar voice echoed out behind them. "Annie?" Annie turned, catching sight of Janis standing by the diner doors. She was out of breath, her hair flying every which way. "Ethan!" Janis ran toward them, hands pulling her purse tighter over her shoulder. "Thank God I caught you. Mind if I... ?" She motioned to the other side of the booth, taking a seat. "Hardgrave told me you were heading out today and I might find you here."

"We like the cheeseburgers," Annie said.

"I just— something's been bothering me," Janis spoke in a flood, her words tumbling out like puzzle pieces that needed sorting. "I've been thinking about it because you said there were three parts to the case. The murder, the robbery, and how you were hired."

"All of which Annie solved," Ethan offered, a little alarmed at where this was all headed.

"Right, of course," Janis agreed. "But something bothered me about the letter. I was so caught up in not being exposed. So worried about my marriage, and the kids—" she waved a hand in the air, "— you said the letter you received was only three words. Like that killer a long time ago?"

"Yes," Annie said, her heart pounding. "It was three words. That's what you sent."

"But the thing is," Janis shook her head. "The letter I sent was longer. It was typed, not handwritten. I wrote it on the computer and I mailed it to you by express courier. I have a copy." Janis reached into her bag, pulling out a typed piece of paper. She passed it to Annie, who collected it like she was moving underwater, her motions slow and dream-like.

Annie and Ethan scanned the page, reading what was present, there. It was a long, typed item listing the events that had occurred in excruciating detail.

"There was a murder committed at Aspen Lane. I have been involved in a great wrong, and would like you to identify the killer," Annie read the letter aloud. "I cannot disclose who the killer was because he will know it's me and come after me. But if you find him via your investigation, it will seem unrelated to my request. Please note your full payment enclosed."

"That's the letter I sent," Janis said. "Is that what you received?"

Annie shook her head. She looked up at Janis in utter disbelief. Ethan's mouth dropped open.

"What does it mean?" Janis asked, eyes wide.

"It means someone switched the letters," Annie answered. "Maybe the Real Estate Ripper himself. Or he had someone else intercept the mail," she turned to Ethan. "He may not have committed this crime, but he's toying with me. He's given us an opening. Ethan— he's still out there. We can find him."

Ethan smiled at her, pleased to see she was back on the case. "Guess this means I'll have to rewrite my report. And you're stuck with me a little longer."

"I hope I'm not overstepping," Janis said, "But Krystal told me when Mr. Markin was murdered she ran her Tarot cards, and she kept pulling the card for 'Justice.' She was afraid it meant she'd be outed for all the money she took. But what if it meant something else?" Janis tucked a stray strand of hair behind her ear. "I mean, Krystal may lie about business, but she *is* a legitimate psychic. Before I met Sheila she told me new love was on the horizon, and she was correct. She told Mr. Markin someone who was meant to be his protector was going to betray him, and she was right about that, too. What if that card Krystal pulled for justice wasn't about her, and she misinterpreted it because she was too focused on her own problems? What if it meant something more? What if it was about *you?*"

The idea struck Annie as a beautiful one. This case was closed, but Annie was leaving with confirmation that there was still a possibility she could right a past wrong. If Mr. Markin's case had taught her anything, it was that the past didn't just disappear. There was always a way to bring justice into the present.

And Annie intended to make sure justice was served.

THE END.

Love Annie Hudson and want to stay on the case? Keep reading for a special preview of "Murder in the Penthouse," Book Two of the Annie Hudson Real Estate Mystery Series. Available now in paperback, ebook, and audiobook!

MURDER IN THE PENTHOUSE

CHAPTER ONE

TONY VASQUEZ DIDN'T LAND with grace when he fell from the balcony of his eleventh floor, ocean-view penthouse apartment.

Hours after he'd taken the plunge, Tony's crumpled form was arranged on the hood of a parked car, where he'd landed with such force the car's front end had caved in on itself. Now, Private Investigator Annie Hudson stood in front of Tony's smashed remains, noting the lack of dignity in his position. One of Tony's arms protruded over the front bumper. A single shoe lay discarded on the pavement. The rest of Tony was buried in the engine well, the fact that he was slightly less visible in such a position his only relief. On this scenic harbor road— marked by soaring seagulls overhead and the light of buildings across the bay— Tony's mangled form was quite a scar.

Annie reviewed what she had already gathered from witness statements about how he had fallen. According to one bicyclist and a pedestrian– both of whom had been touring the harbor at the time– it wasn't a pretty sight. Other victims of falls from similar heights were at least afforded the dignity of a beautiful demise, their arms spread wide like birds in flight, a calm suspension carrying them through their final moments. But not Tony. Tony had flapped his arms in a panic, a tangle of limbs reaching for whatever might stop his descent. His scream was so loud it ricocheted across the night air on this narrow, harbor street in San Diego, and multiple guests at nearby hotels would later claim they heard it with their own ears. He careened through the air like an unwilling bowling ball, his weight dragging him toward the Earth, his fingertips skimming the top of a palm tree as his body landed on a parked sedan with a final, unapologetic thud. The sedan's alarm had blared for twenty minutes afterward, until the owner arrived at a mess of a scene. Police cars. Ambulances. All of them too late to help poor Tony.

"We came here for a favor and you're already putting us to work," FBI Agent Ethan Beckett said, his voice bringing Annie back into the moment. Ethan was standing next to her but also a foot behind, giving her the space he knew she needed. As Annie's only frequent companion, Ethan understood her many quirks— and wanting a comfortable radius of space around her person while she worked was one of them. "Annie said you were a friend, but I'm starting to question if that's the truth." The laughter in his words made it clear no harm was intended.

Beside him, San Diego's Police Chief Melissa Sanchez drank her coffee from a paper cup, unaffected by Tony's crumpled body. To her, this was just another day at the office. "Hey," she shrugged. "San Diego is a busy city for crime. You can't bring the greatest mind into town and not expect us to put it to use."

"I'm surprised no one's settled on suicide as the case's obvious conclusion," Annie said. "No offense meant, of course. It's just—"

"None taken," Chief Sanchez said. "We don't have the bandwidth for the amount of trouble we see. You're right. If it barks like a dog, we're going to call it one. Most falls are jumpers. Plain and simple. I'd bet lunch that's what this is, too. A simple suicide. But his father..."

"Doesn't agree?" Annie asked.

"His father owns the building. He's at the station now. He seems to think this is all tied up in Real Estate. Claims somebody wanted his son's apartment. Suspicious packages had been arriving as well, over the course of many weeks. He thinks it was murder."

"And?" Annie smiled, not one to miss the opportunity to give her friend a needling.

"And," Chief Sanchez ran a hand through her long, waving hair. "Tony's father happens to be a big donor to a certain unnamed elected official's campaign. The same official that appointed me as Police Chief."

"Don't bite the hand that feeds you," Ethan nodded. "Smart choice."

"Look," Chief Sanchez sighed. "Nobody wants to accept their relative was struggling. This, right here?" She motioned at the mess in front of her, eyeing the broken car and the pieces of Tony that were tangled in the engine line. "It's a classic suicide. Open and shut. At the same time, we have to give the impression of due diligence. Meanwhile, I've got other people who need help from us. People who don't have rich Dads. People who are trying to keep their kids outta gangs or getting beat up by their spouses. People with real problems, you see?" She leaned in, her voice lowering. "That's where my heart is. That's who I'm called to help. A case like this is— noise." She waved a hand in the air at nothing in particular. "Still, someone needs to investigate to keep Tony's Dad off my ass."

"And we're the ass-savers," Annie nodded. "Ethan? You up for it?"

"I'm game if you are," Ethan answered. "The FBI has concerns in this area. Lotta trafficking, some DHS action. I can justify the time."

"So, we have a deal?" Chief Sanchez nodded, eager to wrap the meeting up. "I'll tell Tony's Dad we've brought in the world's foremost expert in real-estate-related crime and that you're conducting a thorough investigation."

"You have a deal," Annie agreed. "But I want the scoop on the letter, in return." Annie referenced the reason they'd come to San Diego in the first place. On her last case, Annie had received a letter from an uncatchable serial killer who had been responsible for murdering her brother. The letter was only three words long, but the way Annie had received it told her the killer had access to internal police information. "He was waiting," Annie added. "The person who sent the letter. He was waiting until a case came up that involved my specific niche. Real Estate. He knew before the FBI, which means he's someone on the inside. Or he knows someone on the inside. He watched the cases as they came in—" Annie trailed off, unwilling to say more.

"It'll take some time," Sanchez warned. "Thousands of departments out there. You'll need to let me make some calls."

"We've waited fifteen years," Annie answered. "I'm here for as long as it takes." She paused, thinking of her friend's safety. "You'll want to be discreet. He could be one of your own. It would explain how he's evaded being identified."

"Don't you worry about me," Chief Sanchez smiled. "I can handle myself. We have a deal." Chief Sanchez extended a hand and Annie shook it, the two women striking a deal based on mutual respect and necessity.

"Now," Annie leaned down, staring at Tony like he was a friend, her eyes pained. "Let's find out who killed Tony."

"You don't think it was a suicide?" Chief Sanchez balked, a little annoyed at Annie's resistance to entertain the most obvious of answers.

"No," Annie shook her head. "His father is correct. He was murdered." She looked up at the tall building in front of her, from which Tony had fallen. It was an eleven-story, upscale apartment building, perched on the edge of the water. San Diego was one of the world's most expensive cities, and real estate like the building in front of Annie was half the reason. Double doors marked the entryway, modern pillars holding up an awning with the building's name written in pretentious script: *Rowling Heights.* From its lofty upper floors, the best units in Rowling Heights overlooked the San Diego harbor, their occupants privy to a secret cycle of orange sunsets and yellow dawns. Across the harbor, moored sailboats bobbed up and down, their sails tucked safely away in case the wind picked up. An occasional seagull made its way toward the edge of the harbor's defensive cliffs. To the East, a collection of similar buildings reached for the sky, the lights of their windows steady and sure. Their noticeable opulence and the gentle hush of waves drove home the point: living at Rowling Heights meant more than an apartment. This place wasn't just a location. It was an *experience.* One worth paying for. And Tony? He had paid with his life.

"I'll need to speak to the residents," Annie said. And with that, her investigation began.

To continue reading, purchase "Murder in the Penthouse," Book Two in the Annie Hudson Real Estate Mystery Series! Available now in paperback, ebook, and audiobook.

MORE FROM VALERIE BRANDY

The Annie Hudson Real Estate Mystery Series:

- "Murder in the Penthouse" — The Annie Hudson Real Estate Mystery Series, Book Two.
- "Murder on the Farm" — The Annie Hudson Real Estate Mystery Series, Book Three.

The Predator / Prey Thriller Series:

- "Trail of Obsession" — The Predator/ Prey Thriller Series, Book One.
- "Lies Run Deep" — The Predator/ Prey Thriller Series, Book Two.
- "The Trap is Set" — The Predator/ Prey Thriller Series, Book Three.
- "The Woman in the Wind" — The Predator/ Prey Thriller Series, Book Four.

LETTER FROM THE AUTHOR

Dear Reader,

Thank you for dedicating your time to the world of Annie Hudson and the Real Estate Mystery series! I'm a screenwriter and filmmaker coming to books from Film & TV, but one thing I love about books in particular, is connecting directly with a community of readers. It's very special to be able to speak with you and hear what you want from characters in our novels.

I hope you'll reach out to me by joining my mailing list at the link below! I love to keep my readers updated on new releases, offer advanced copies, free giveaways of novellas, sneak previews, and more.

If you liked Annie Hudson, I hope you'll keep reading the rest of the series, which continues to grow! In addition, my "Predator/ Prey" thriller series is available now in all formats, starting with book one, "Trail of Obsession."

And if you want to read more from me in general, I hope you'll check out the list of my books on the previous page.

Warmly,

Valerie Brandy

Join the author's mailing list at:

www.valeriebrandy.com

ACKNOWLEDGMENTS

To God, and the energy of all that is good in the universe.

To my Mom, family, friends, and creative muses.

To the readers, who are always on my mind.

To the author community, who is shaking things up.

www.ingramcontent.com/pod-product-compliance
Lightning Source LLC
Chambersburg PA
CBHW030138010826
48973CB00002B/622

9781964161136